TRINITY ICON

a Charlemagne file

K.A. Bachus

Cover by Marigold Faith

CHARLEMAGNE FILE TIMELINES

Short Story Collection
A Lighter Shade of Night,
mid 60s to early 70s

Novels
Trinity Icon, early 70s
Cetus Wedge, early 80s
Brevet Wedge, nine months later
Lion Tamer, five months later
State of Nature, early 90s
Vory, a year later
Swallow, five weeks later
Quiet Move, late 90s
Goat Rope, 1999

CONTENTS

PROLOGUE

Tsaritsa lingered in every breath. Sweet, aristocratic, it was Mara's favorite incense. She closed the church door behind her. Her left arm tingled, aching, warning her of death that day. She ignored it. She did not need that arm to cross herself as she kissed the icon of Saint Sergius. She would not need it for the dusting, or the polishing, or the sweeping. It was a little sore, that was all, and these old bones had known soreness before.

It took time to find where the Matushka had hidden the supplies. The woman was not very organized. Not that it is easy to be organized with four young children. Easy, no; necessary, yes. Mara offered to do this Monday's cleaning instead of watching those children for the Matushka. It was the least she could do—the very least. The very least she could get away with after seeing the unruly crowd of small bodies in the Matushka's living room.

Mara stood among the saints with a duster in her hand. They gathered around her, smiling at her from their windows to the Kingdom of God. She turned slowly and smiled back at them, at their places on the iconostasis before the altar and on the walls and stands around her.

What a life I have had, thought Mara. I would just as soon start over as to finish it. Is that possible, God? She shuffled to the Icon of Christ the Pantocrator, crossed herself in the prescribed manner, and kissed it before dusting it. All things are possible with God, but I doubt He will let me start over. And because I doubt, He certainly will not.

Mara did not often think deep thoughts. They were dangerous and useless and she had given up all attempts to understand such things long ago, on the death of her third child. Faith was her support and her only weapon, faith in God, distant and unknowable, faith in the Church, a haven, a comfort, a system of salvation, and faith in every mystical possibility ever presented to her. Superstition ruled her reason. It was rare for her to doubt. It was more rare for her to understand.

Her faith gave her great comfort through the years. It brought her through the purges. It brought her through the Great Patriotic War. It brought her through the searing pain of great loss, year after empty year. It did not, though, improve her discernment of either the finite or the infinite. She had seen enough of the finite to know she was not particularly interested in seeing it more clearly. But something nagged at the back of her awareness, telling her she was missing the mark in her search for the Almighty.

Missing Him or not, she continued her lifelong struggle to approach. She was as much a part of the Church of Saint Sergius as the icons and candles. She could be seen, at Vespers, during Royal Hours, throughout the Sunday Liturgy, lighting candles or crossing herself quickly, three times to everybody else's one. Straight, coarse streaks of grey hair escaped in thin tufts from under her black shawl and fluttered in the breeze created by her mobile right arm. Her thin lips moved soundlessly with the droning Slavonic chant of the choir—whether it was present or not. Today it was absent. It was Monday and she was alone with the saints.

As she reverently dusted the icons on the north wall, she stopped before the Trinity Icon, where another old woman, Sarah, laughed at the message three angels were giving her husband. She dusted Sarah while pondering the second coming.

I am becoming quite a thinker. I wonder if my children will be all grown up. If they are, they will be perfect, won't they? Then how will I know them? And how can it be heaven if I have missed them growing up? If they are little, how can I raise them as old as I am, or will I be young again? And Kolya, will he be young or old? How would he have looked in his old age?

She remembered a game they played before the children came. They had only an hour or so every day before his parents came home from work. The apartment was so small and crowded, it was difficult to get around obstacles. But after making love, they would arm themselves with two perfume aerators left to Mara by an ancient babushka who had known an easier time. There was no perfume in their corner of Stalin's Russia, even if they could have afforded it. Instead, they filled the fragile relics with icy water, and, naked and giggling, chased each other around that small space, hiding, seeking the advantage, spraying, and shrieking as the cold mist found its mark. When they had exhausted themselves and their bottles, they would collapse, damp and panting on their narrow bed for a last cuddle before polite tapping at the door announced that his parents were home.

Mara smiled at the memory. She replayed it in her mind, substituting her own now-aged body, and imagining Nickolai as he might have been in his old age: balding like his father, somewhat potbellied, but still vital, still laughing. The revised memory widened her smile. As her memory extended in time, she succeeded in misting her husband's narrow, hairy behind, and she broke a fifty-year silence.

Her cracked, cackling laugh sounded strange in her ears. Stranger still was the answering chuckle from just above her right shoulder.

ONE

My Darling Daughter,
I know the recruiters have contacted you, and that you are considering entering the game. I know because of the questions you asked me this holiday. 'How did you meet Daddy?' was artless and cute when you were five. At eighteen, it takes on new meaning.

Of course, they want you for your education and your facility with languages, but there is also the matter of your pedigree. I don't think, in all these years of your training, that anybody has explained this to you. I will do so now, with more detail than my usual "I met Daddy in Chicago."

I tried to teach you what I know about the next world and the things that have been proved necessary for getting there. I have also given you basic skills for living in this world, in the civilized, sunlit world, where you have, for now, the privilege of going to school.

The others have taught you, and taught you well, all the necessary family survival skills for the black world, where secrets are both weapons and currency. Of course, these skills do not merely protect you in our world; they also draw you into it.

Heredity counts for nothing in the face of free will. Your inheritance is only another gift to be used or rejected. But the recruiters think they want you for it. Even if whatever genetic combination you are were immaterial to them, they would want you for your family connections. These remain, no matter what or who you are. There are people who love you, and, the recruiters believe, will do anything for you. I hope to give you some idea of what 'anything' can be—another subject where your training has been vague.

In writing this, I had to step back in time within myself. Memories tend to be two-dimensional—black and white newsreels without emotion—but what I have to tell you is about an event in my life that involved all of me. I've tried to tell it so that you will not only understand but also feel a little of what I felt then, which I think is the principal intent of any writing. I have the advantage of distance in time so I can be more objective than I could have been twenty years ago, but your father was my beloved, remember, and I miss him still.

No document can fully reveal the living man, despite the faith bureaucrats place in their reports. Still, your recruiters don't have any of this in their files, nor should they.

I did try not to, but I know I've allowed a few words of advice to creep in here and there—and one or two lectures. I am a mother. I cannot resist giving advice. Here's the first piece of it, no doubt unnecessary: Do destroy this when you've finished reading, won't you, dear?

Your loving mother,
Alexandra

TWO

I was born and brought up in Chicago, a first-generation American born to Russian immigrant parents. My father was a salesman or something and was gone most of the time until I was fifteen, when he had an accident that hurt his leg and forcing him to retire. His early retirement put us in a poor financial position, and I struggled to go to college.

We lived on the south side, near 87th Street and Cicero Avenue, in a plain brick box of a house built in the 1960s. It was different from the others on the block only because it had a chimney; my father insisted on having a fireplace in the living room. The neighborhood was on the very edge of the city; the south suburbs began across 87th Street. It was an urban residential place, missing both the dynamism of downtown Chicago and the serenity of rural Illinois.

For three years after high school, I lived at home and commuted to school. I majored in Chemistry at the Illinois Institute of Technology on 31st Street near the Dan Ryan Expressway. I earned a few small scholarships and worked every third semester to make up the gaps in tuition. Everything worked out until I began to concentrate on my major.

It seemed that as my coursework became more demanding, so did my mother. I finally came to a difficult decision, financially and otherwise, and left home on a Wednesday during the first semester of my third undergraduate year. I had to leave. Life in my parents' house was intolerable and I could not study. My mother, God rest her soul, was impossible to live with and we were having a blow-up on average once a day.

I remember my father standing in the doorway of my basement room, surveying the open suitcase and two cardboard boxes that held all my belongings.

"Anything I can carry up for you?" he asked.

I nodded, checked the closet again, and closed the suitcase. Papa left with a box, reappeared, and silently lifted the other box. The stairs creaked beneath him on the landing, echoing in the empty room, disturbing the silence of the house—a void silence, caused by the absence of noise, not the presence of peace. I took the suitcase off the bed and followed my father upstairs.

Outside, our goodbyes were sparse. "How about coming for dinner on Sunday," he said. "For your mother's sake."

"I thought she never wanted to see me again." I read the desperate warning look he gave me. "Okay, Papa, I'll be here."

He closed my car door, ignoring the rust chip that fell on his shoe. Stooping to look through the window, he said, "By the way, Father Paul wants to see you. He called while you were packing."

"Why?"

"He didn't say. Just stop by before you go... home."

Home. It lifted the tension a little to know that my father, at least, accepted my leaving as a natural progression, not a betrayal.

I drove an old Volkswagen Beetle at the time—very old. It ran well (when it ran), but it was not aesthetically pleasing to look at. People had a hard time deciding what color it was, and it had several nasty habits, like occasionally—make that frequently—refusing to start. I drove it out of love and poverty.

That day, the Volkswagen started on the third try. I ground it into an uncertain forward gear and lurched ahead, too busy trying to see the road through a scratched and dirty windshield to acknowledge Papa's melancholy wave.

THREE

My old bug tick-ticked up the steep driveway of the priest's house, shuddered, coughed, and died ten feet from where I wanted it to stop. I left it in gear, set the parking brake, and waited for it to finish rolling backward another five feet before stepping out.

Father Paul's wife, Erin, answered the door looking a little less harried than usual. She was a first-generation American like me but from a large Irish family. That she was now the Matushka of a Russian Orthodox Church was a testimony to love and the American melting pot.

"Hello," I said.

"Hello."

We stood at the front door looking at each other, locked in the kind of mutual unseeing stares that afflict people who are absorbed by their own affairs.

I forced myself to speak. "Papa said Father Paul wants to see me."

"Oh." Erin gave a rare smile and moved back from the door. "Come in."

Two red-headed bodies, three feet high and moving fast, hurtled past me as I stepped over an assortment of trucks and toy dishes.

Erin did not seem to notice them, nor did she make any attempt to stop them as they dashed screaming down a hallway to the left. She pointed toward the right, "He's in the dining room," she said. "Go on in."

The 'dining room' was the window end of a long, narrow kitchen. It doubled as Father Paul's office and was partitioned from the kitchen and open-plan living room by two patterned curtains. On the near curtain, rectangles in graduated sizes and shades of purple drew the eye toward the floor where an old green carpet in the living room met the yellow tile of the kitchen. The other curtain was either uncertain brown or faded purple, with only a hint of a former pattern. The arrangement did nothing for the room but proclaimed, rather loudly, a lack of taste and money.

The room would look much better without those awful curtains, I thought. I was more convinced of this when I stepped behind them and had to raise my voice over the din of the children to get Father Paul's attention. If this ugly partition was meant to offer privacy, it failed.

The priest looked up from a blank pad of lined paper. Several wadded balls of the same paper were strewn across the table. His expression, in contrast to his wife's, was more haggard and worried than usual.

"Alex! Thank you for coming so quickly. I need to speak with you."

"Good morning, Father." After kissing his hand, I sat down in an uncomfortable chair next to him. "She's called you then," I said.

"Who?"

"My mother."

We exchanged puzzled looks.

"Has she?" The priest seemed startled with sudden understanding. "Oh, yes, she has. But that's not why I asked to see you."

His expression turned inward again, and I was struck by the toll the struggle was taking. Paul Strukov was only in his thirties, but dark circles under his eyes and a permanently worried expression added ten years to his appearance. His struggle was not only financial, though money problems were real enough. I suspected that if this were the only problem, Father Paul would bear his poverty gladly, rejoicing in his weakness as did his eponym, the Apostle. But the gnawing sorrow came from the sad state of his congregation, not his bank balance. On the previous Sunday, I had realized suddenly that I was the only person between the ages of ten and forty who regularly attended the Divine Liturgy. Old women brought their grandchildren to church. No one else had time.

The priest picked his words carefully. "I want to ask your help. It's a little delicate. I mean, I don't want to accuse. It's...."

I said nothing, giving him time to think. With a sigh, he continued.

"The Trinity Icon has been stolen. It's gone, and I think I know who took it. I'm asking you to help me get it back."

"The what? Which one? Do you mean the one with Sarah and the three angels?" I briefly wondered if he was accusing me.

"That's the one," he said. "It's very valuable. Yesterday, someone offered me twenty thousand for it. It was written for Tsar Michael, you know."

"No, I didn't know. Did you sell it?"

"Oh no! I could never sell that icon."

"But it would solve a lot of problems. You could get the church roof repaired, fix up the house a bit...." I stopped for fear of implying that I thought his house needed fixing, though it did.

"Yes, I know, but that's not important now. What's important is that when I walked the man to his car...."

"Which man?"

"The man who offered to buy it." Father Paul paused a moment as if he were finding his place in a rehearsed narrative. "Yesterday, when I walked him to his car, four or five boys suddenly scattered from the south wall of the church. They were spray painting it. With obscenities."

"And when you went back it was gone?"

"No, it disappeared later, sometime last night. But I've thought about it, and those boys must have been near the window when we were discussing it. I had opened it for some air, and well, they could have heard his offer. And when I turned him down, they may have thought…"

I waited, but when he didn't continue, I said, "What did the police say?"

"I haven't called them." He hurried to explain: "I don't want… I recognized one of the boys and I don't want to take a step that may damage him forever."

"Who?"

"Boris Nikitin."

"He's no boy."

"Well, he's young. He can change. He can't be twenty-one yet. A lot can happen to a man…." An inward look suggested the priest was speaking from experience.

"He's older than I am and I'm twenty. What do you want me to do, Father?"

"Talk to him."

"What?"

"Talk to him. Mention that I haven't called the police yet and that if it's returned, you know. No questions asked. That sort of thing."

"Why are you asking me?"

"You know him. You went to school with him."

"We went to the same high school, but I certainly don't know him."

"You're the only person I know who can approach him without it looking strange."

I did not tell him how mistaken he was. I looked at his anxious face, sighed, and said, "Okay, Father, I'll try."

"Great! I knew you would." Relief brightened his features for a moment.

The cloud returned, though, when I said, "So, what did my mother say?"

"When?"

"When she called."

"Oh, the usual. She asked me to tell you to go back home."

"Are you telling me to go home?"

"No. Do what you have to do. But be kind to her, won't you?"

"Of course." My voice rose in bewilderment. "Why do some women get that way, Father? I don't remember my mother being so bitter when I was a child."

The priest shrugged and changed to a more comfortable subject; he had had his fill of difficult topics that day. "How's school by the way?"

"It's fine." But I was not so easily put off. "I had to move out, Father. Finals are in three weeks and I can't study at home. You do understand, don't you?"

"I do, but your mother doesn't." He sighed and stood up, stretching his arms from the shoulders in the half-hearted manner of a weary man. "Are you sure Sizzle Burger will hire you again next term?"

"They always do. Two terms on, one term off. It's worked for three years now."

"Yes, but can you afford an apartment as well?" He pulled back a curtain. "It seems to be taking you long enough to finish school without adding this expense."

"I know what I'm doing." I immediately regretted my unthinking reply to the good man, especially because he was right and I knew it. In three years, I had barely completed two years of college.

We walked to the front door, picking our way around and over trucks, balls, books, and dolls. Erin was playing patta cake with her youngest. She did not notice that I was leaving.

The beetle started the first time. I let it roll backward down the drive, then began the struggle to find first gear. I noticed Father Paul saying something to me from the doorway. I shook my head. He repeated it, but I could not hear him. I cut the engine as he ran up to the car.

"Just wanted to say thank you again," he said.

"Oh. No problem, Father. I'll do my best."

The priest walked back up to the house, stooping to collect a toddler that had escaped through the open door. I sat, blocking two lanes of traffic until the bug started again on the fourth try. As it lurched into first gear, the traffic jam re-solved itself in front of me, and several cars fell into line be-hind. Among them, though I didn't pay attention to it at the time, was a light blue Rambler car, slightly dented. I remem-bered it later when I had reason to. It followed me to my apartment, parked across the street, and did not leave again until the last of my boxes had been unloaded.

FOUR

It was Saturday afternoon before I could keep my promise to the priest. I knew where Boris would be. I found him where he spent most of his waking hours, in a rundown restaurant across the street from the high school. Two years after leaving (not graduating) school, he still sat in a corner booth, nursing cokes and pots of coffee, making each dollar last two hours, meeting a dwindling roster of his contemporary cronies, and coaching a growing number of younger admirers from the high school.

I approached his table, sat down opposite him, and was granted an audience. After explaining myself and asking a few questions, I was convinced of one thing: Boris was far too stupid to steal a twenty-thousand-dollar icon.

"You know," said Boris, "You're not as ugly as you were in school, man. I bet if you took off them glasses, you might even..." He reached across the table. "Naw. I guess not."

I retrieved my glasses from his dirty paw and wiped at the greasy thumbprint he had left. I succeeded only in smearing it, sighed, and put them back on. I had begun to slide out of the booth to get away from this bum as quickly as possible when I realized someone was standing beside our table.

"Vasily, my man!" said Boris with what seemed forced enthusiasm.

"Hello, Nick," said the man. I detected an accent even in these two words, and for a moment wondered who was Nick.

"Hey, siddown, man," said Boris. "Don't mind the ugly broad. She's just leaving." To me, he said, "So I don't know nothing about no icon, okay? See ya."

Having resolved the origin of "Nick" in "Nikitin," Boris's last name, I turned my attention to this man, Vasily. He was, even through the haze of one greasy lens, magnificent. Everything Boris was not, this man was. He was muscular, well-dressed, and seemed intelligent.

"Icon?" He stared at me intently.

I melted.

"Yeah." Boris leaned toward me. "Scram, Sasha," he whispered.

"No, please, don't leave because of me," said the stranger. He sat on the booth seat next to me, effectively preventing me from going. He regarded me with penetrating light grey eyes. I noticed that two fingers were missing from his right hand. It seemed to be his only flaw. His jaw was firm, his features even, he was almost thirty. I was flustered and immediately infatuated. I struggled to maintain some dignity.

"Sasha," he said, "Are you Russian, then?"

"No," I managed to squeak. "I'm American. Please call me Alex." I immediately regretted the automatic response, registering his Slavic brow and accent and sensing that he might be offended. He did not seem to be, though, so I asked, "Are you Russian?"

"No." He did not elaborate.

"What icon is it that you know nothing about, Nick?" he asked Boris.

"Oh, I dunno. Some icon's gone missing at St. Sergius' Church. I told her I don't know nothing. I ain't even been in there in ages. Listen, about that guy you asked me about...."

"What icon is missing, Alex?" Vasily asked me.

I stumbled over every other word of explanation. I was puddled and incoherent under his gaze, wishing my intelligence would present itself and draw his attention away from my unruly hair and big nose, knowing it never would unless I could get hold of myself. I was in agony as I heard my voice screeching, tried to modulate it, forgot half of what I meant to say, said the other half stupidly, and finally gave up without saying much of anything.

"Is it valuable?" he asked.

"Yes. Someone offered Father twenty thousand for it the day before it was stolen."

"Twenty grand!" Boris was suddenly interested.

"Who?" asked Vasily.

"I don't know." I began to recover as it occurred to me that there was a lot I didn't know. The exercise of mentally listing the questions I needed to ask Father Paul restored me to my usual distracted state and I did not immediately notice the intensity of Vasily's stare.

He made me notice it though, when he began asking me questions about myself. His gaze seemed to search me; his questions probed me. His apparent interest in me struck something deep inside that I had not known was there. This had never happened to me before and it deepened my first infatuation.

Vasily was soft-spoken, understated, but in a way that suggested tremendous power, as if he were accustomed to having his way. His spare conversation did not come from reticence; it came instead from an expectation of obedience and the self-assurance of a man with control over himself and others. He seemed to have a wry sense of humor as well. He spoke to Boris in circles, while he questioned me directly. He made Boris uncomfortable and appeared to be enjoying it, in the way a cat plays with a mouse before killing it, as an interest in life, a natural way to have fun before serious business begins.

When I told him I was a Chemistry major, Vasily became more animated, brought out an expensive pen, and began writing, left-handed, equations on a napkin. I was in my element now, and we had fun with combinations. He was an expert chemist.

He asked what my last name was, and I told him breathlessly hoping yet disbelieving that such a man could be interested in me. His reaction when I answered was striking. He seemed disturbed and uncomfortable and gave me a piercing stare as if I had insulted him in some way.

"I am sorry I have kept you," he said, rising abruptly. "It was nice meeting you, Alex, and I hope I will see you again."

I did not see how this was going to be possible. Although I had answered his questions about many things, I hadn't told him where I lived and he never asked me for my phone number. I didn't have a phone, but I was disappointed he didn't ask.

"I will talk to you later, Nick," he said to Boris.

"Sure." Boris watched him leave.

I wanted to watch Vasily, too, but Boris drew my attention instead. There was something in his expression, something I didn't understand, servility, certainly, nervousness, yes, and... fear?

FIVE

I mmersed in the splendor of the Divine Liturgy at St. Sergius's on Sunday morning, I set aside all earthly cares, and thoughts of my mother, Vasily, Boris, and Boris's insults. For an hour and a half, I deliberately did not look at the conspicuously empty spot on the north wall where the Trinity Icon had been. I waited until after the final blessing to study it. My mother's continued refusal to speak to me gave me time to look at it closely. I was grateful.

I could picture the icon that was missing. It had been one of my childhood favorites. I remembered gazing at it during the long chants of the Liturgy. I could see it in the candlelight of the Liturgy of the Presanctified Gifts during Lent. It spoke to me of joy, humor, love, and the power of God.

Sarah stands in her tent, laughing, as three angels tell Abraham that Sarah, well into her nineties, will have a child. She laughs at the thought of an old woman pregnant and for the joy of having a son, for the love of her husband, and for the love of God who would bless them so. She is completely human in a divine circumstance, laughing at herself as she bows to the will of God.

The colors were still vivid after almost four hundred years, the gold more valuable than ever. The icon consisted of three pieces, two smaller sections hinged on either side of a large middle section so that the icon could be closed. Closed, it would be three feet square, too large to be inconspicuous. Opening it added another three feet to its width.

"I think your mother wants to talk to you," Erin said, interrupting my study of the blank wall.

"No, she doesn't. She's not speaking to me."

"She keeps staring at you." Erin tried to shake off the four-year-old tugging on her skirt. She did not succeed, and another child attached himself to the other side.

Erin reminded me of a walking beehive. Her children hovered around her, buzzing.

"I'll talk to Mom later, at dinner," I said. "You're looking rather happy today."

"Happy? Well, yes, I suppose. I'm always happy."

Maybe, but then you hide it well.

"It's a shame about poor old Mara, isn't it?" said Erin.

"Mara?" I searched the few remaining people gathered at the door, looking for the old woman who had been as much a fixture in that place as the icons. "Where is she? She wasn't here today. Is something wrong?"

"She's dead."

"Dead?"

"Died Monday."

Father Paul walked over and whispered something to his wife. She moved away with two in tow, scooped up a third, and told a fourth to follow her. The child complied by running around her as she made her way to the door, completing the beehive effect, and leaving the church behind in comparative silence.

"Did you talk to him?" asked Father Paul.

"Yes, Father."

"And?"

"I'm sure he doesn't know anything about it." I hesitated, looked at the worried priest, and asked, "Can I ask you a couple of questions, Father?"

"Sure." His word was open, but his expression had closed.

"How did the thief get in?"

He shrugged. "Picked the lock, I suppose."

"It was locked then?"

"Of course." He seemed distracted.

"And the windows?"

"No sign there."

"You have the only key?"

"No," he said with great patience. "The Parish Council president has one, but he's been in Florida for two weeks."

"One more question—no, three more. First, who offered to buy it?"

"I don't remember his name, but he gave me his card." Father Paul searched his pockets. He opened his wallet and handed me a business card. "Do you want it?"

On the one hand, though I had been asked to help, it wasn't any of my business. On the other, I was curious. I took the card. The name on it did not begin Vasily.

"Second question," I said, "Was his the first offer you've had?"

"For this icon? Yes. I'm negotiating several offers for others, but none of them are nearly as valuable."

"Others? You're selling others?"

"Yes, the Council decided it was the only way to raise the money to fix the roof before it falls in."

"But you turned down this…" I looked at the card, "this guy Brent Grayson. Surely the sale of one icon would have taken care of everything."

"Not that icon."

"Why not?"

"I can't. I won't sell that icon. Some things are more important to this church, to my work." His expression closed more than ever. "What's your third question?"

"My third? Oh, yes. Who else knows about the offer? Who have you told besides me?"

"Nobody." The priest thought for a moment. "I did mention it to the bishop's secretary that evening at my house. But he wouldn't have had time to tell anybody else before it went missing. He didn't leave my house until after ten, and the icon was gone by six in the morning."

"The bishop's secretary! Why was he here? Is the bishop coming?"

"You said three questions, Alex." He covered this evasion with a smile. "We'd better get some coffee before it's gone."

...

That afternoon, I had dinner at my parents' house. When I climbed into my old Volkswagen afterward, I hugged the wheel before trying to start it. Dinner had been a disaster. The first course consisted of a long sulk seasoned with sighs of martyrdom. Next came a rushing stream of hysterical accusations, half in Russian, half in English, covering every misdemeanor I had committed since the day I stopped wearing diapers. For dessert, there was a virulent curse topped by a violent door slam. I did not stay for coffee.

The street lights had just come on when I parked in front of my studio apartment. I walked upstairs, unlocked my door, and stepped from the bright hallway into the sepia gloom of the apartment, navigating by memory across the room to turn on a light. I had turned on the light and put the kettle, full and sizzling, on the tiny stove before I noticed Vasily sitting on the sofa bed in a shadowy corner, watching me silently.

SIX

My apartment was on the third floor of a block-style brick building near Pulaski Road. It consisted of one room and a bathroom. The room was divided by a short counter that created a kitchen nook with a two-burner stove, sink, and small refrigerator. This was the view as the door opened, and where I had first concentrated my attention when I came in, as there were two leftover slices of pizza in the fridge that could, maybe, erase an empty dinner.

I was not used to having strangers waiting for me in my apartment, sitting on my sofa.

To the right of the door was the bathroom. To the left was part of my furniture, a stack of planks and cinder blocks that made a system of shelves to support my stereo and books. Across the room from the stereo was a sofa bed, where Vasily sat, one arm casually sprawled over the top while the other held a magazine in the fading light from the only window on his right. The window looked out onto the street. In front of Vasily was a small, plain coffee table Papa had found in the attic and let me have.

I stood with my mouth open, trying to find words to fill the space.

He said simply, "Hello."

When I was still mute after a long pause, he said, "I came to see you, knocked on the door, and it opened as I knocked." He stood and walked toward me. "I came in to see if everything was all right and decided to wait for you."

I recovered. I felt a cold shiver spread through me as I faced the intruder calmly, my initial infatuation dissolved by his lie. The door had not been open. My disordered appearance disguises an orderly mind. I have a system for everything, from putting books on a shelf to locking my door. I have never locked myself out of home or car, have never lost a document, and have never discovered a forgotten item in the bottom of a drawer. I catalogue, group, classify, and place each item in my life with unsparing precision. I do this without descending into obsession because my rationalism is simply a natural result of the way in which I think, and it causes problems only when I am forced to live with someone as chaotic as I am systematic. Like my mother.

I faced Vasily and for the first time understood that he was dangerous. The knowledge cleared my mind and allowed me to think and to watch him carefully.

"Did you find your icon?" he asked.

"No," I said. "Why? Did you?"

"I am not looking for it."

"But you're interested in some way."

Vasily looked at me with a different intensity. I watched his eyes move from my frazzled, unkempt hair, to my perpetually wrinkled wool skirt, and back to my face.

"You are not what you seem," he said.

The kettle whistled wildly, billowing steam. "Coffee?"

"Yes."

"Why are you here?"

He took a moment to reply, so I had time to look up from the stove to see his expression. He seemed to make a decision. "I came to ask you to have dinner with me."

Another great lie.

"I don't know you," I said.

"Nick introduced us."

"Who? Oh, Boris. He's hardly what I would call a reference. I don't even know your last name."

"Sobieski."

"What's a Pole doing with a Russian name?" I handed him a coffee mug.

"Sobieski is Polish."

"Vasily is Russian."

"Poles use it."

"Obviously."

"I did not know Americans worried about such things."

"I'm not worried. I'm curious."

"That appearss to be your biggest problem."

Our conversation continued this way until the coffee was gone. We answered questions obliquely or not at all and circled each other in a verbal contest for advantage. With difficulty, we agreed to meet at a restaurant of slightly better quality than Boris's hangout.

I was not sure how I should feel about this milestone in my life. On one hand, I had just made my first date. He was not just any date, either, but a handsome, apparently wealthy man who radiated power and self-assurance. I was uneasy though, because I could not believe such a man would be interested in me, and I knew instinctively that he was accustomed to having his way.

For some reason, he kept bringing the topic around to my parents. Where were they and who were they and did I know where they were from? I answered simply 'Leningrad' since this was what I had been told. I was on my guard with this man and unwilling to say more to him.

"Do you believe in coincidence?" he asked me, finally getting the hint that I did not want to talk about my family.

"It depends on what you mean," I said. "If you mean do I believe that coincidences happen, yes, I do. I think there is plenty of evidence. But if you are asking if I believe in pure chance, no, I don't."

"Precisely."

"Which?"

"There is no pure chance," he said. "A coincidence happens because someone causes it to happen."

"Yes."

"There is always an explanation."

I was not sure what he was getting at. "No," was my answer. "There is not always an explanation."

"There must be. If there is a cause, it can be explained."

"Not necessarily," I said. "The cause can be the primary cause of all things, who requires no explanation. Even where there is a surface, or human, explanation, if you trace it back as far as it will go, you come to the primary cause."

"God?"

"Yes. Of course."

"Are you going to preach to me now, Alex?"

"No, why?"

"Are you devout?"

"What does that mean?"

"Even if one allows that God is the original cause, there is still a natural explanation. Don't you agree?"

"No, I don't," I said. "God is not bound by natural laws. He can do things directly, without using natural forces."

Vasily looked at me strangely. "If there is a God, and if He is interested enough," he said.

"There is, and He is."

Moses' tongue was loosened when he required it. Not mine. This was the best I could do. I can sit in an easy chair and conduct brilliant philosophical arguments with myself. But as I sat next to Vasily that day, engaged in a conversation I was having difficulty following, logical argument failed. Faith cannot be shared by logic.

"If He is interested," said Vasily, "then it is in a general way, not individually."

"I disagree," I said.

"What is your argument?"

"My argument lies in the word coincidence. To coincide means to exist or happen at the same time. Do you accept Einstein's theory of relativity?"

"Yes."

"Then you accept that time is relative."

"Yes."

"Then for events to coincide within the infinity of time, yet each within its own relative time, requires direction from outside of time."

"Or chance."

"No. Not chance. Coincidence is common to the human condition. Everyone experiences it. Its frequency suggests a cause greater than chance; its universality means it is individually directed."

"I don't agree," he said. "Universality cannot mean individuality."

"Then what is your argument?"

He seemed distracted and did not answer. Instead, he changed the subject and we had another cup of coffee. As we talked, I had the impression he distrusted me. He seemed forever trying to catch me at something, but I did not know what. Our conversation ranged over many things, his arguments always well defined, and his insight better than mine, especially regarding people. He avoided philosophy though, and kept the topics centered on the concrete.

After an hour, my infatuation returned; he was fascinating. But I did not forget how he must have come to be there. It sobered me and made me careful.

"Saturday, then," he said, draining his cup. He stood to leave. "I will pick you up."

"No," I said. "We said we would meet."

"Oh, yes. That's right. I will see you then." He walked to the door and seemed bothered by something.

I went with him to the door, hoping with everything in me that he would kiss me. He didn't. I was bitterly disappointed. He unlatched the deadbolt lock with some expertise and let himself out.

Once he was gone, my disappointment gave way to a desire for security. I attached the chain lock, knowing it was useless, and searched for something to put against the door. There was nothing heavy enough to hold it so I settled instead on an alarm and piled several pots precariously under the doorknob. Safety provided for, I rushed to the window to satisfy my curiosity. I reached it in time to see Vasily climb into the passenger side of a black Mercedes parked under a streetlamp.

SEVEN

O n Monday afternoon, when I should have been attend-
ing a physics lecture, I approached instead a large
glass building gleaming in the center of a crowded parking
lot. I found Grayson's suite on the second floor, entered
through a door labeled Grayson Antiquities, Inc., and stumbled gracelessly to a stop in front of a manicured, but vapid,
receptionist.

"Is Mr. Grayson in?" I asked.

"Do you have an appointment?"

"Uh, no. I was in the area and thought he might see me.
If I could just ask a question or two…" I glanced nervously at
my reflection in the mirrored wall behind the receptionist.
The image did nothing to encourage me.

"What is this regarding, please?" she said.

"An icon. At Saint Sergius."

"Just a moment."

I glanced at my reflection again and tugged at the front
of my suit. I can take a designer suit and make it look like it

came out of a garage sale. And this was no designer suit. Frump, I thought. That's me. What am I doing here?

"He'll see you now."

"He will?" Recovering from the surprise, I tried to assume a more dignified demeanor. The mirror showed me a frump trying to look dignified. I gave up the effort and rehearsed the questions I wanted to ask Grayson. The receptionist led me to the polished mahogany door of his office.

Grayson opened the door and held out his hand. "Mrs. Strukov. You found it!" he said. It was a statement, not a question.

This threw me off momentarily. "Uh, no. Sorry." I shook his hand. "My name is Alex Dolnikov. Father Strukov asked me to ask you a few questions."

"You're not Strukova?"

"No."

"What's the priest want to know?" He waved me into the room and indicated a chair across from his desk. "Come in; come in and sit down."

"I have just a couple of questions."

"You said that. What are they?"

I watched him as he walked to the window on my left. Balding, thin, with a large nose and a prominent Adam's apple, he reminded me of a vulture. He hung his predatory head over the sill and surveyed the parking lot below. He was very thin, almost emaciated, but his office was opulent, every item expensive and self-indulgent. Cut crystal jars of expensive candy graced every flat surface. He paced from one jar to the other taking liberal samples.

His nervousness must keep him thin.

He did not stop moving. With each mouthful of chocolate, he returned to the window. I had just cleared my throat to ask my first question when he stopped by the window and suddenly bent lower over the sill, staring at a point in the traffic below. He spun furiously and faced me, glaring.

"Who sent you?" he demanded.

"I...." I did not have an answer. I had sent myself, actually, after it was no longer my affair. I had done my part by talking to Boris, now I was being a busybody. But I couldn't stop. Too many questions tugged at me, demanding answers. I was nosy. I admit it.

"What do you want?" he demanded again.

"Just a question."

"So ask it!"

"You offered Father Strukov twenty thousand dollars for the Trinity Icon."

"That's not a question."

"Did you?"

"Yes."

"And he turned you down?"

"Yes, damn it."

"Were you expecting him to accept?"

"Of course I was. We were supposed to close the deal, weren't we? Look, you tell him," Grayson turned briefly from his minute study of the parking lot. "I'll go twenty-five, but that's it. That's as high as I'll go."

"He told you he'd sell it?"

Grayson looked at me suspiciously. "I thought you said he sent you?"

"He did. Sort of. Did he say he'd sell you the icon?"

"Yes."

"When?"

"Monday." He tore his eyes from the window again and gave me a narrow look. "What do you mean, sort of?"

I ignored the question and rose to leave. "So he said yes on Monday but no on Tuesday?" I asked, backing toward the door.

Grayson advanced a few steps, studying me. "That's right," he said. "It's Charlemagne, isn't it?"

"Who?"

"You know who. I know and you know and you tell those spooks not to worry. I'll have the money before tomorrow. Tell them. You got that? Tell them."

"Sure. I'll tell them." I hadn't the faintest idea what he was talking about, but I found his company unpleasant and was anxious to get out. I stumbled again on the doorstep, recovered, and walked away quickly. I was almost out of the building when I heard him calling behind me, "Tell them!" I turned and saw that he had followed me down the stairs from his office suite.

Once outside, I ran to my car, praying it would start the first time. It did and I lost sight of Grayson as I sped through the sprawling parking lot.

I reached the adjoining street and turned right, not noticing the light blue car turn behind me. It was small and innocuous and meant nothing to me. I did notice the black Mercedes behind it, though. It was distinctive, and I had seen it before.

EIGHT

Though I noticed and recognized the Mercedes, I did not seriously believe it could be following me. I knew Vasily was interested in the icon in some way, but I assumed he had come to see Grayson, and I expected the Mercedes to park in the lot. I was surprised, then, when it was still two cars behind me at the on-ramp to the Dan Ryan as I drove to school.

Surely there is no reason to follow me. He knew where I lived, and I told him where I went to school.

My exit was coming up. As an experiment, I drove past it, watching the rearview mirror. There was no hesitation from the Mercedes. On impulse, I crossed two lanes and took the next exit suddenly. The Mercedes was still one car behind me. I was so fixed on it that I continued to not notice the small blue car between us. I began to panic and did not register the anomaly of two cars following me through otherwise deserted streets in a rundown industrial area of the South Side.

The tame tick-tick of my Volkswagen's engine became a wild scream as I pushed the gas pedal to the floor. I tore my eyes from the mirror and found myself heading into an abandoned warehouse area. It was a desolate place, several blocks long, bounded by scrap yards and boarded-up buildings, the only deserted and wild space for miles. *You fool.*

The Mercedes moved up behind me. I took a gentle curve in the road without skill, skidding more than turning, but managing to stay on the pavement. As the road straightened, the Mercedes moved into the oncoming lane and accelerated.

The next curve defeated me, and my Volkswagen fishtailed from side to side as I struggled with the wheel, gripping it knuckle white, almost giving myself up to wholesale panic. A flash of blue passed by my left elbow. My wing mirror was filled with a black reflection bearing down on the left rear fender. A van appeared in the oncoming lane. As the Volkswagen's rear skidded toward the right shoulder, the Mercedes clipped the front left fender, hooking it and dragging it forward, and changing the direction of its spin.

The tearing metal and boom of contact were whispers compared to the roar of the van that screamed by me within centimeters of my nose, its horn blaring. It took another moment for my car to stop—on the sidewalk, facing the opposite direction. I wasted no time. Shaking hands ground the starter, forcing a spark. The Mercedes was not in sight as my beetle sputtered and whined back down the road in second gear.

I drove to school and decided to collect myself at the library, hiding between two rows of shelves containing the ancient philosophers. I took Plato from a shelf and sat down with him at a small table in a private corner. Opening the book in front of me for camouflage, I put my head in my hands and tried to stop shaking and organize my thinking.

Mental organization did not help the situation. My parents' home was severely uncomfortable and my apartment now felt unsafe. My car was badly damaged; the left front fender had peeled back as if iopened with by can opener, and the wheel shimmied strangely. Even if I could find the money to fix it, which I couldn't, it would take days in any shop, days I would have to skip class.

My grades so far that term were no better than my finances. This was the buckle-down part of the term, the latest point in which I could start paying attention and maintain my A average. I did this every term. I began by doing nothing, or as near to it as I could. I studied only enough to get a maintaining grade on the midterm, then three weeks before finals, scrambled to catch up. By finals week I was ready, having expended no more than four weeks of effort during twelve weeks of school. Of course, the last three weeks were intense, but for some reason, I had to flirt with failure to generate any ambition. I am not recommending this, you understand, and I hope you have more wisdom in this area than I had.

Finals were two weeks away. Father Paul's icon had already taken more time than I had to give, and I did not think my car's left front wheel would last to the end of term. The recent possibility of physical danger receded in the face of certain academic disaster.

"I'm in over my head this time," I muttered.

"Are you?"

He was sitting in the chair across the table from me, wearing a suit this time, with a tie and vest that made him oddly out of place in an academic environment. His coat bulged open as he leaned casually back in the chair, revealing to my angle of sight the edge of something underneath, a black strap of some kind, a bulky outline. I thought I knew what it was.

Intellectually, I knew I was in danger. Emotionally, I did not feel it. I feared finals week more than the threat sitting across the table from me. Simple humility, a rare enough virtue in me, convinced me that I was not important enough to warrant the attention of anyone too dangerous. Vasily was either interested in me and harmless, which seemed unlikely, or dangerous but disinterested.

Either way, despite all I knew, despite my rational analysis and attempts to interest myself in the possibility of running, I could not move. Maybe my body was still moribund after the energy it had consumed on the road. Perhaps my will was sapped by the prospect of academic ruin. Whatever the reason, I did not run.

I also did not properly observe the man in front of me. I mistook the accusation in his expression for indifference. I thought the irony in his words came from boredom. I ignored the bulge under his coat and chose not to see the steadiness with which he stared at me.

I surprised myself with an angry, impatient response to his question. "What's it to you?"

"It depends," he said, "on how your mistakes affect me."

"My mistakes?" I struggled to keep my voice from shrieking. "Affect you? You have some nerve! You're responsible for it all and you have the nerve to..."

I was too enraged to notice his expression grow even colder. I was not pierced by his stare, nor did I appreciate the sneer with which he answered me.

"And how am I responsible for what you have done to yourself, little girl?"

"Done to myself?" *And don't call me little girl.*

I could not believe it. "I did not run into myself on the road, Mister. I did not chase myself and wreck my only means of transportation to school two weeks before finals. I did not do that, Mister!"

Vasily's sneer remained, but his brow furrowed, as though puzzled. Suspicion was still first in his tone, though, when he said, "Chase yourself? Are you accusing me? I did not chase you."

"I know perfectly well that you drive a black Mercedes. You nearly killed me."

"If I meant to kill you, Alex, it would not have been 'nearly'."

I shivered. His words, his attitude, were becoming clear to me. "Why did you chase me? What do you want?"

"I did not chase you."

"It must have been you."

"Where were you and your boss going?"

"My boss? What boss? I don't work during school terms."

"Your boss. Do not lie. You went to see him. You both came out of the building, and he followed you from the parking lot."

"Who followed me?"

"Do not act stupid with me, Alex."

I tried but failed to understand. "I don't have a boss this term. And you're the only person I know with a Mercedes."

Vasily put one hand to his forehead in a gesture of frustration. "Listen. I was in the Mercedes. Your boss was in the other car. Your boss, the man you are working for."

"What other car?"

"The blue car."

"There was a blue car?" I replayed my memory of the chase. I could not see a blue car but sensed the presence of other traffic. But my boss? Who?

"I'm not working for anybody. Honest."

"You are trying to find an icon." He said it slowly and distinctly, the way a teacher would explain a lab procedure to a dull student.

"Do you mean Father Paul? I'm not working for him...."

"You are very good, but now you are overdoing it."

"Overdoing what?"

"Pretending to be stupid."

"I'm not pretending. Believe me. I've never felt so stupid. I don't have the foggiest idea what you're talking about. I have six finals to take in two weeks, a car with a bent wheel and no fender, no money to fix it, and no vehicle to replace it, and you're going on about Father Paul in a blue car." I slammed the book down in front of me and began to get up. "I've had just about...."

Vasily's grip on my arm stopped me. It was a peculiar grasp, made with his right hand, the one that was missing the last two fingers. It should not have contained all the power of a whole hand. But it did, and it levered me irresistibly back into the chair. He leaned across the table and said, softly, carefully, "Whom did you see today?"

I saw the connection. I finally noticed the blue car in a mental replay of the afternoon jaunt about town. "Grayson? Brent Grayson? You were following him? He happened to be behind me, and you were following him! Well, that's a relief." I got up again to go. I was levered back down again into the seat.

"He did not 'happen' to be behind you." Vasily released my arm, leaned back in his seat, and studied me. "He was following you, or you were leading him."

"Leading him? Where?"

Vasily did not answer.

"Look. I'd like to understand it all, but I don't have time, and it looks like it would take a very long time to explain. I don't know when to butt out, that's all. Father Paul asked me to talk to one person. I got curious and talked to another one. I hereby officially declare that I am no longer curious about any icon. I quit. Leave me out of it, OKAY?"

Again, he did not answer.

I ran my fingernail down the corner of the book, making a ratchet sound. I looked at him again, noticing for the first time how cold he was, and that he did not believe me.

He broke the silence. "I will take you home."

I did not like this idea, but he gave me no room to protest. He led me from the library with sure authority, swiftly through the front doors, down the steps, and across the now-darkened street. He opened the front passenger door of that black Mercedes, helped me in, and closed it behind me. I heard a lock catch. There was no light in the car when the door opened. Nor was there one when Vasily opened the back door and slid into the seat behind me. I could see the outlines of two other men in the car, one in back, the other beside me, driving, but I did not see their faces until they were illuminated by the bright lamps overhanging the northbound entrance ramp to the Dan Ryan.

"This is not the way to my apartment," I said.

NINE

"*Erstens essen wir,*" said the driver next to me.

I understood this. Four years of high school German left me competent in simple conversation. I almost replied in the same language, but something stopped me. Vasily knew so much about me, did he know this, too? Or was this something I could keep from him, possibly to my advantage? I knew I was going to need any advantage I could get. Thought and decision took only a moment. "I don't understand," I said.

He said we will eat first," said Vasily. He leaned forward from the back. "We know a quiet place where we can talk."

I hoped they did not notice my shudder. I did not want these men to know that I feared them because I had decided to base my defense on ignorance. 'Talking' did not sound like a pleasant prospect.

"Misha's English is not very good," said Vasily. "Is there another language you can use that we all know?"

"No. Sorry."

"What about Russian?"

"Sorry. I don't know Russian."

"You must know Russian. Your mother is an émigré. Surely, she taught you Russian."

I groped for a response. "I'm not fluent. My Russian is practically useless. My mother gave up on me years ago."

"Good. We'll use Russian." Vasily leaned back in his seat.

The decision had been made, but no language was used for another half hour. The car made its way across the city with silent occupants. Enveloped in a luxury I had never seen before, surrounded by men I instinctively knew were not safe, I felt small and insignificant, imprisoned in a fast-moving cage of power and wealth, in circumstances I did not understand.

After one of many turns, the car glided down a curving driveway in front of an older building, not as tall as the sky-scrapers crowded around it, and stopped under a long awning that stretched from the front door of an exclusive restaurant. A uniformed footman reached for my door, but Vasily jumped out of the car and helped me out before the man could reach the handle. I thought of screaming but had no time to decide. I was marched into the building quickly, Vasily gripping my arm tightly, while the other man who had been in the back seat walked ahead to make arrangements for dinner.

We were shown to a table immediately. It was the only table in an elegant little room. *How nice. How private!* I debated the possibility of running out of the room. But I could be mistaken, imagining things. Wouldn't I look a fool running out of a posh restaurant in downtown Chicago? And then where would I go? How would I get back to the South Side at that hour? I didn't even have a dime for a phone call.

Our table was centered in a semicircular booth, very cozy. I was helped into the right side of it; Vasily sat on my left, his arm around my shoulder. The other two men blocked the left end of the booth to my right. I considered slinking under the table, but Vasily held me very close, so close that I could feel the gun under his coat, the one I had guessed at in the library. He was letting me know for sure. Threatening without speaking, smiling at me. I returned to ignorance as best defense and pretended not to notice. I smiled back at him.

The third man explained to me in passable Russian that this was his favorite restaurant in Chicago and would I please allow him to order for me. He introduced himself as Louis, said proudly that he was French, and treated me to a light conversation that I found easy to follow. He was gallant, jolly, and warm. He had dark curly hair and darker eyes that changed intensity according to the subjects we discussed, none of them important. I began to like him and to doubt I had any reason to be afraid. Then I glanced at the driver, the man Vasily called Misha. I noticed his expression as he filled my glass again with the incredible wine we were drinking. Chateau something, by Rothschild somebody. Like liquid candy. Not a hard, too sweet, obvious candy, but a subtle one, warm, enticing, and melting. Misha watched me carefully, and I remembered that I was afraid, there was reason to be, and I had decided to pretend that I wasn't. This was not difficult, since the wine was affecting me, making me warm and comfortable despite my grim situation.

But I did not like Misha. He had a polished and beautiful exterior that nonetheless suggested hidden menace. Like an iceberg, he seemed most dangerous beneath the surface. He was as handsome as the other two and maybe more, blond, blue-eyed, well built. Unlike them, there was nothing likable about him. His stillness was immediately chilling, his politeness clipped, form only, devoid of the human compassion that originally spawned all forms of etiquette. One would not forget such a man, but one would want to. He did not look at me, he looked inside me. Even more, he invaded me. My response was instinctive. The more he probed, the more I did my best to conceal. He gave me more than a few mental shudders.

A young guy in a suit came to the table and spoke to Misha in German. I pretended ignorance but was able to catch most of it.

"Who is the girl?" said the man.

"You tell us," replied Misha.

"Frank will want to know what you're up to. What should I tell him?"

"Tell him I sense a threat that I will take care of."

"I am not so sure," said Vasily. "She may be what she appears to be." (This was not very clear to me. My grasp of the conditional and subjunctive was, and still is, shaky at best.)

"Let's not be hasty," said the man. "Let me see what Frank has to say." He turned to me and asked in English, "May I ask your name, Miss?"

"Alexandra Dolnikov."

He repeated it and left.

The man's visit seemed to mark a change in the atmosphere of the little room. Louis's charm and the warmth of the wine receded before an onslaught of questions from Misha. His questions were politely phrased, in perfect Russian that was nonetheless not native to him, but each made me tremble. He knew much already, but I could not be sure how much. I did my best to appear thick, innocent, and uninvolved, without actually lying, since lies create a labyrinth that can be deadly to the liar.

"Vasily says you are looking for an icon," he said. "Have you found it?"

"No." I risked a few more words. "I'm not looking for it. I told Father Paul I would talk to Boris Nikitin about it. He thought Boris might know. That's all. Really."

"Have you known Grayson long?"

"I don't know him," I stammered. "I... Father Paul said he offered to buy the icon, so I asked Mr. Grayson some questions. That's all. Really."

"Why did the priest ask you for help?"

"Oh, I don't know. Because I went to school with Boris, I suppose."

"Why did he tell you about Grayson's offer?" I shook my head. I did not understand.

He put on his worst 'being patient' look. "You are twenty years old. Why are you, of all people, trusted with such things?"

I had no answer. Why does anybody tell somebody something, anything? What makes people drop bits of information, as though leaking them from a bucket, for others to pick up willy-nilly? And why do I pick up and keep all those bits that are dropped in front of me?

"What did Grayson tell you?" came the next salvo from cold corner.

I was still wondering how I had come to be young and trusted at the same time, so this question caught me off guard. I answered it automatically. "He said, 'Tell them I'll have the money tomorrow. Tell them.'"

Louis broke the tense silence after a few seconds. In German, he asked Misha, "What do you think?"

"She is lying," said Misha.

It sounded like a death sentence, and I involuntarily blanched. Misha, who was watching me carefully, noticed and raised his eyebrows in surprise and recognition. His meaning could not have been clearer if he shouted it in perfect English. He had not known I understood German, but he knew now. And he considered it proof I was lying.

Before I could further incriminate myself, a short, round man with bulging eyes came up to the table. He spoke to Misha. "She's clear."

"No, she is not."

"As far as we're concerned, she is."

"But it is my concern that counts most here."

"Yes, well, let me see if I can cool the situation, all right?"

Misha answered with an icy stare.

The new man was slightly nervous but seemed to know what he had to do and was determined to do it. He turned to me. I was comforted by the coffee stains on his shirt and tie; it reminded me of my dad.

"Miss Dolnikov, my name is Frank Cardova. I'm sure you'd like to be going, wouldn't you? May I take you home?"

"Yes, please." I whispered it.

Nobody moved. Frank Cardova stared back at Misha. The room seemed filled with explosive vapor, waiting for a spark. It was the moment of disaster when silence gives the boundary between peace and violence.

But the moment passed. Misha gave the slightest nod to Vasily, who left his place and extended his hand to me, helping me, almost pulling me out of that booth. Cardova propelled me out of the restaurant in much the same way that Vasily had dragged me in. After my initial relief, I wondered if I was wise to trust yet another man I had never met. I looked at his receding hairline. He would eventually be quite bald. Papa is certainly not bald, I thought, and he is older, so why does this guy remind me of him?

"What the hell were you doing in there, young lady?" he asked me when we were safely in what I guessed to be a rental car on the way to my apartment.

I wanted to say 'trying to stay alive', but I was still not sure about this man. "Having dinner," was all I could say.

His googly eyes swiveled off the road and onto me. "I see," he said. "Bit of a daredevil, are we? Like taking risks? Why not get a burger and eat it on a subway track during rush hour?"

"Who are you?" I asked. "And who are those guys?"

"I told you my name and those guys are poison. Stay away from them."

"I know your name, but what are you? Are you one of them?"

And why are you so much like Papa?

"I'm their babysitter, so to speak. I'm not one of them, but I am beginning to wonder what, exactly, you are."

"You all seem to know everything. I don't know any-thing."

"That's a very good policy," he said. "I advise you to stick to it."

"I will. I'm through with this… whatever this is."

"Glad to hear it, now tell me all about it, my dear."

"I said I'm through."

And I'm not your dear.

"Just tell me everything—the truth."

His voice carried a note of authority, again like your grandfather, so I told him.

"So Grayson thinks it's him and he thinks it's the money," he said when I finished, more to himself than to me. "That one's a bad egg, young lady. Stupid move on your part, going over there. You drew a lot of attention to yourself."

"Grayson thinks what's the money?"

"Nothing. Don't worry about it."

I tried a different tack, curiosity and a sense of security momentarily pushing my earlier resolutions aside. "Is it money?"

"No, of course not." Cardova was again speaking more to himself. "He owes some people a lot of money and thinks he can save himself. He's wrong. They aren't the people and that's not the reason."

He drove and I watched the city slide by until we were parked in front of my apartment. I had not told him where it was. I was beginning to wonder if there was anybody who didn't know where I lived.

"Listen," said Cardova, "Those guys are hazardous to your health, eh? Especially Grayson. Don't go near him again."

This was a surprise. "I thought Grayson was pretty harmless. I mean, compared to Misha."

"It all depends on the circumstances. Grayson's are desperate and he knows it. That makes him dangerous and unpredictable. Nasty combination. Plus, you never want to stand around at the target end of a firing range, and that's what I'd call a twenty-five-foot circle around Grayson right now. Misha, as you call him, is just plain dangerous, but predictable. Everything he does has a reason. I'll do what I can to keep you out of his sights. You do your part and you'll be all right."

"So who is Charlemagne?" A sudden memory brought it to my mind; impulse asked the question.

In the light of the street lamp we were parked under, I could see Cardova's surprise. "Where did you hear that?"

"Grayson said it. Or he asked it. He said something about 'it' being Charlemagne."

"Did you tell them that?"

"No. I just now remembered it."

"Well, forget it. Completely. Wipe it away. Don't ever say the word again. Got it?"

"Got it."

TEN

I was feeling particularly secure the next morning as I
sipped my coffee. There was no Mercedes outside. My
pots and pans intruder alarm by the door was undisturbed.
Frank, the dear, wonderful man, had solved things, and I
was determined to take his very good advice. Safety was attractive today.

As I surveyed the pans by the door, I noticed for the first
time a note lying on the floor. Father Paul had arranged a
meeting at his house with my mother and could I please
come over before going to class? No, I could not. No car. No
phone. No finals. No future. Safety was suddenly not
enough. There were other problems to solve.

I managed to call the priest from a pay phone down the
street. He said he would pick me up and take me to school
after our meeting. I dreaded this meeting and would have

been glad of any excuse to get out of it. But his offer of a ride to school was a temporary fix to an immediate problem.

In Father's house, the ugly curtains were drawn back, combining the dining room with the living room and improving the look of the whole place considerably. Mama waited for us, having coffee with the Matushka. The two women sat at either end of the table, watching absently as a chaotic and noisy jumble of little bodies hurled themselves and their toys around the living room.

Erin stood and offered me her chair. Father Paul took a side chair while his wife made more coffee.

"Father, I know you mean well," said Yelena Dolnikova, "but this daughter of mine wants nothing to do with her own mother."

"Mama, I'm right here. You can talk directly to me."

"Why should I? You never listen."

"I do listen—when you have something to say."

"I always have something to say."

"No. You're always saying something. It's not the same thing."

Unsurprisingly, this infuriated Mama. She became temporarily speechless, a rare condition.

"Now then," said Father Paul. "Why don't we try to find some common ground, a starting point for understanding? You two cannot go on hurting each other this way."

"There is no common ground." Mama said this before I had a chance to say it.

"Yes, there is. We must find it." Turning to me, the priest asked, "Why did you move out, Alex?"

"I have explained that to her ad nauseam."

"Explain it again, Alex."

"I don't want to hear it," said Mama.

"Please, Yelena Alexeievna, just a little while. Please," said the priest.

I felt the bitterness rise in my throat as I remembered what it had been like at home. The priest's presence barely helped me resist the urge to list my mother's offenses and come directly to the point. "I can't study at home, Mama."

"Why?" It was not a question. It was a confrontation. "Tell me why."

"Because you won't leave me alone." I could not contain my exasperation any longer. My reserve faltered, and I spewed it all out, word after word, hurtful or not, not meaningful as a whole except in the emotions expended and the pain perceived.

"Because I can't go anywhere without you following me around. I can't sit with a book. I can't have silence and peace. It's one stupid conversation...."

"Stupid!"

"Yes, stupid. One after another. No proof of anything, but you accuse everybody of everything, and I'm tired of hearing it. But that's still not it. It never stops. I get up in the morning, and you're talking. I go to bed. You're talking. Same topics. Same people. Mara did this. Mara said that."

My voice had risen considerably so that it did not have far to go to become a scream. "I don't care what Mara said."

"Well, she said it on her deathbed. I thought you would like to know. You never listen!" Mama was also shouting.

"I don't want to know! May her memory be eternal, she was a crazy old woman. I never believed a word of anything she said."

"You have no respect for the dead or for your elders. You know nothing. She suffered much. She had real wisdom."

"What?" I accepted the cup of coffee Erin offered me. "She shut out everything new. She was mired in superstition."

"New is not always good."

"It's not always bad."

"True. But you are no judge."

"I'm a better judge than you think, Mama."

"She said what on her deathbed?" asked Father Paul. "When did you see her, Yelena?"

"Just before you came, Father. I saw you pull up to the hospital as I was leaving. I waved. Didn't you see me?"

"No. What did she say to you?"

"She told me about the icon."

I was suddenly interested. "What about the icon?"

"Now you're interested. You couldn't be bothered on Monday night, sitting there with your fancy notebooks and drawing numbers and letters like some secret language. It's that ancient alchemy is what it is. It will lead you to perdition! A wise old woman lies dying in a hospital and you don't want to know about a miracle."

I groaned. "Not the miracle again."

"Yes, again. No, not again, because you never listened the first time. You don't really believe."

"I do believe, Mama. I just don't trust Mara's interpretation. There's probably some explanation. What's the miracle?"

"Even when there is an explanation," interrupted the priest, "It can still be a miracle."

Erin refilled his cup. "I agree with Alex," she said. "There is always an explanation, usually somebody's imagination."

"I didn't say always," I said.

"You've given birth four times and you don't believe in miracles?" Mama asked Erin.

"No, I don't. I don't see that mess out there as a miracle." Erin pointed to the living room.

"Well, it is. You just don't know how to discipline your children, that's all."

I put my head in my hands and waited for the explosion set off by my mother's wayward mouth.

"You have your nerve telling me how to raise my children," shouted Erin above the din. "You don't know what I put up with!"

"I do know. I've been there. What you put up with is what you get."

"My children won't leave me."

"But you'll want them to!"

"Mama," I said, "What was the miracle?" It was the only thing I could think of to stop the shouting. Father Paul's "Now, now," was not working.

"What miracle?"

"Mara's miracle."

"Oh. The icon, the Trinity Icon, laughed. Sarah laughed. With Mara! Mara was thinking about her late husband—you know he died in the Gulag. Mara thought something funny about him—she wouldn't tell me what—and she laughed, and Sarah laughed with her. Imagine it! The icon laughed. We have a miraculous icon. Isn't it wonderful?"

"That's not entirely accurate."

"What? You don't believe it? Well, Mara heard it and I believe her."

"I'm sure she did. I find it easier to picture the icon laughing than Mara with a smile on her face. No, I mean it's not accurate because we don't have the icon, miraculous or not." Turning to Father and cutting off Mama's next comment, I said, "Did she tell you about her miracle, Father?"

"Yes."

"On Monday?"

He nodded.

"You believed her. Didn't you?" asked Mama.

The priest looked distinctly uncomfortable. He shifted in his chair and stared into his coffee. "No," he admitted. "I didn't."

Mama's eyes opened wide, shocked, horrified. Erin, who had been noisily shifting dishes between the sink and cabinets, became still.

Father Paul continued. "But I was in the church the next evening. I was to meet someone there, as I explained to you before, Alex," he said with a confidential look. "I was contemplating that icon when it struck me, just as you mentioned, that it must have been something to see Mara laughing. The thought made me chuckle." The priest looked into his coffee again. "Then Sarah chuckled, too."

"So you turned Grayson down."

"I had to. I couldn't let that icon go. Where would it wind up? No matter how many assurances he gave me that it would go to a private collector, what if it were placed in a museum? On a wall next to who knows what? Think of the people in this church, the people who should be in this church. I could not let go of a miracle."

A loud crash of a frying pan into the sink signaled a renewal of the Matushka's efforts to express herself without speaking.

"You told the bishop's secretary," I said.

"Yes. We drew up a plan to try to verify the miracle."

"You would have looked like a fool," said Erin.

"I would not have, Erin. I am no fool and the bishop knows it." He sighed and slumped in his chair. "But that's neither here nor there now that it's gone."

"Like my little girl," said Mama. "My little girl is gone, too. The icon will turn up, Father. You've mislaid it. But my little girl?" She gave me a pleading look.

"No, Mama. I'm not a little girl, and I have to make my own home."

"You will always be a little girl to me."

"I know. That is part of our problem. You don't see me as a person."

"I do see you as a person."

"If you do, it's a person you made up. Your idea of me has nothing to do with who I am."

"I know more about you than you think. You forget, I made you."

"God made me."

"He gave you to me to finish and polish. I do know you. If there's something I don't know, it's because you never bother to tell me. You keep your life away from me like you're afraid I might steal it."

"You don't give me any space. You want to know every-thing. Can't I have some privacy?"

"I don't want to know everything. I just want to protect you. I want to tell you what I know so you are not hurt. Don't you understand that? Where is your car? There is an example! What has happened to it? Do you have any idea how much it hurts not to know?"

"The car broke down, Mama. That's all."

"What will you do now?"

"I'll manage."

"How?"

"I'll think of something."

"That's it. You will think of something." Mama threw her hands in the air. "Don't ask for help. Don't relieve your poor mother's mind. You will probably hitchhike or something. Some nut will pick you up...."

"I won't hitchhike. But I have to make my own way."

"The way is a lot harder than you think." Mama stood up. She picked up her purse and walked to the door.

"I'm a lot stronger than you think, Mama."

"Yes. I know you think so. Goodbye, Father, Matushka." She let herself out, slamming the door as her goodbye to me.

...

I watched the traffic around us as Father Paul took me to school. There was no sign of a black Mercedes, but I realized I felt torn between regret for the absence of Vasily and relief at the absence of Misha.

ELEVEN

My last class that day was Physics. The book was ponderous but the professor made us bring the thing to class. So I was saddled with it all day, along with three notebooks, a lab book, a three-ring binder, and my purse, a large bag-like affair that, collapsed and mostly empty, hung on my shoulder. I left the physics building and took a shortcut to my car, walking behind the math building toward the library parking lot where my crippled beetle squatted, looking dejected. I hoped I could make it limp home, where I would make a decision about our futures.

It had been a grey day, with a drabness that dampened color and sound. In the late afternoon, the dim light faltered in an early sunset. Nothing was distinct. The lines of buildings, landmarks, trees, and signposts were smudged in a watercolor dusk. There had never actually been daylight that day, only a lighter shade of night. Full night was returning, creeping along the narrow lane I walked on. It hid the tall man until he was right in front of me so that I had no warning, and no opportunity to run.

"I have to talk to you," he said.

I could not, at first, remember who this was. I peered through the gloom trying to see his face. The voice was American. He was too tall to be Frank Cardova.

"Did you tell them?" he asked.

It was Brent Grayson.

"Tell who?"

"You know who."

"Tell them what?"

"The money." He dragged the word out, with forced patience, his teeth clenched.

"Oh. Yes. I did."

"What did they say?"

I tried to think, tried to remember every word said, every expression. My only distinct memory was my fear.

"Nothing," I told Grayson. "I don't think they said anything."

"Well, here. Give them this." He handed me a large brown paper bag.

I protested, not least because the bag was heavy and I had enough to carry.

"Take it. Give it to them. Give it to Charlemagne. See, here's the money. They can go back where they came from."

"Money?"

"Fifty thousand. No! Don't open it here. It's all there, don't worry. Tell them to go away."

"That's not the reason," I muttered.

"What?"

"Somebody told me you're wrong. Somebody said, 'They aren't the people and that's not the reason.' So take this back."

"What the hell are you talking about? Who said that?"

"I don't know, and I don't want any part of it. You take this back. I've had enough."

"Oh no you haven't," he hissed. "You'll take it to them or I'll find you. You got that? I don't care what the reason is. There's fifty thousand dollars in that bag. It ought to be enough to buy them off. Take it. Tell them if they want more, I'll double it. Got it?"

I shrank from the menace in his face and voice. "Got it," I whispered. I was saying this a lot lately, without getting anything more than a very uneasy feeling.

Grayson returned to the shadows; I could hear his footsteps on the pavement, walking quickly at first, then breaking into a run.

I walked a few steps, trying to balance the bag of money on top of my books. It slid to the left, threatening to fall. It slid to the right. "This is not going to work," I muttered. I dropped the lot and stuffed my books into my purse. One notebook had to be folded to fit. The others stuck out at odd angles, making the purse hang awkwardly on its one long strap. I put the strap on my shoulder. It slid off and the heavy bag thumped to the ground. I adjusted my balance, grabbed the paper sack, and was halfway to a standing position when I realized someone was standing in front of me again.

"Gimme the money," he said.

I looked up, still in a crouch, the heavy purse dangling from my left shoulder, the paper bag in my right hand. I saw a head silhouetted against the distant glow of the parking lot street lights. The hair was long and unkempt. A knife poked at me from the shadows, barely illuminated by the walkway lights behind.

I shuffled slightly to the left, to make him turn his head so I could see his face. The knife followed me, coming closer.

"Gimme the money!" he insisted.

It was Boris. I could see him now. I could also see the parking lot to the left. There were no obstructions. I could run, but weighed down as I was, he would catch me. I could not bear the thought of giving way to him. He was so low. He was my ideal of the despicable. I did not fear him because he was so contemptible, a fawning braggart, no brains, no courage, but plenty of ambition. My mind worked for a way to disappoint him as if this were only a mildly interesting puzzle.

"Come on. Gimme it."

"I can't. It's for Vasily."

"I know that. I was watching Grayson for him. Gimme it and I'll give it to him."

"Will you?"

"Sure."

"I'm not so sure there is money in here, though," I said doubtfully. "I was just looking in the bag, and it looks like just some wrapped packages. Is that how they wrap money?"

"What? Lemme see." He stooped as I brought my left hand to the right to open the paper bag. The movement started the strap of my purse sliding toward my elbow. I moved my left hand as if to stop it, but instead grabbed the strap and changed the trajectory of the swinging purse so that it swung up toward his head. The edge of my physics book caught his right eye; his head snapped backward and he fell heavily.

I ran to my car without pausing to look back. I checked the mirror as I searched for my key. Nobody coming. I found the key, but it would not go in. Tearing my eyes from the mirror to look at what I was doing, I took the key out of the light switch and put it in the ignition, checked the mirror again. Still nothing. Turned the key. Nothing. Pumped the gas pedal and turned the key again. A reluctant cranking sound. A figure emerged from the side of the math building, staggering. I turned the key again; the Volkswagen started; it limped from the parking lot, making scraping noises and pulling stiffly to the left—with me chuckling at the wheel.

TWELVE

I made it to the 87th Street exit before the left front wheel fell off. Still several miles from my apartment, I started walking. After an hour, both shoulders ached from alternately carrying the book-filled purse. My feet hurt and I was hungry. I stopped on a busy street corner, well-lit and bustling, hoping for a sign of a bus stop. I found one, but the last bus had run fifteen minutes before.

My aching feet and shoulders did not concern me as much as the fact that I was about to enter an unwholesome neighborhood alone, at night, carrying fifty thousand dollars in a brown paper bag. When Vasily pulled up in front of me, then, I was not faced with a choice between safety and danger, but between dangers known and unknown.

I looked at him. He did not look sinister sitting alone in a small boxy red car. I looked past the street lights at the dark avenue stretching before me. He had never actually threatened me, had he? I was probably imagining things when I thought there was a gun under his coat. Frank's words receded in a hazy recollection of some marvelous wine. Didn't

I still have a date with this guy for Saturday? He was my first date and I was afraid to get in a car with him?

"Get in," he said.

I got in.

The car was new. It smelled new. Everything on it glittered. There was a sticker in the window.

"New car?" I asked.

"Yes. Do you like it?"

"It's nice."

He looked at me as we waited for the traffic light to change. "You do not like it."

"I do," I insisted. "It's just, well, it's not you, is it?"

"Isn't it?"

"No. It's a girl's car." I glanced at him as the light changed and we began to roll forward. "Is it your girl-friend's?"

He did not answer for a moment. I could not tell if it was because he was deciding what to say or was too busy trying to find the next gear. He was unfamiliar with the car. "Look in the glove box," he said.

The temporary registration was in my name. My name, my address, my social security number, my driver's license number, my date of birth, my height, weight, color of hair and eyes, all typed in neatly, accurately, precisely.

"You forgot my hobbies, dreams, aspirations, and what I did in the second grade," I said as I put it away and turned off the map light.

"Pardon me?"

"Nothing."

"This is to replace the car you say I destroyed."

"Thank you. But I can't accept it, you know."

"It is your car. You must accept."

"I can't."

"Why?"

Because ladies do not accept expensive presents from men. Because it's a form of selling oneself. But he hadn't asked for me. It seemed a bit presumptuous to think that he would. He had wrecked my car, and this car was registered to me. It wasn't as if I could walk away from it without anyone noticing.

"How do you know so much about me?"

"I know only the surface things."

"Isn't that enough?"

"We'll see."

He was semi-communicative. I risked another question. "How did you get into my apartment the other day?"

"I told you."

"You told me a lie." I surprised myself with this little spark of courage.

He was surprised, too. "How did you know?"

"I don't forget things. I don't lose my keys, and I always lock my door. It's a talent of mine. So how did you get in?"

"Louis taught me how to open locks. Yours is ridiculously easy. I had no trouble."

"Louis opens locks?"

"He can open anything."

"Sounds like he's very talented."

"We are all very talented in some way, Alex."

"What's your talent, Vasily?"

I did not expect an answer to this question and I did not get one.

He pulled up in front of my apartment building and set the parking brake.

I could see his face in the street light and decided to risk one more question, to see his reaction. There are times I can't resist doing things like this. In school, I had a furious urge to pull the fire alarm, just to see what would happen. I finally pulled it one day in the fourth grade. I learned my lesson about fire alarms, but I still pull them figuratively now and then.

"What's Misha's talent?" I asked.

"It is not a name you are privileged to use," said Vasily.

"I don't know him by any other name," I answered.

"You do not know him."

"Then what should I call him when I refer to him?"

"You should not refer to him." He looked at me intently. "Or me, or Louis." He climbed out with difficulty and walked to my side of the small car, opening my door for me. He was such a gentleman.

I looked him in the eye defiantly.

"You are reckless," he said.

"You don't have to walk me to my door. I know the way."

"Don't be silly."

As we entered the building, I could smell somebody's dinner cooking. The aroma reminded me how hungry I was. I struggled up the stairs with my purse and bag of money, considering how to get rid of Vasily and the money quickly enough to attack the leftover pizza in the refrigerator. I turned to him at the door with my key in my hand and a rehearsed speech on my lips. He knocked softly. It opened, and he ushered (pushed) me in.

Vasily locked the door behind me as I stared mutely at my one-room apartment. Louis stood at the tiny stove, cooking. Misha sat on the sofa with a paperback. The stereo played Sibelius. Both men had their coats off, guns in full view. They looked very much at home.

THIRTEEN

"Why are you trembling, Miss Dolnikov?" Misha asked it, in German, as he set aside the book.

I tried to stop shaking. The heavy purse slid from my shoulder to the floor with a thump. "I'm not trembling."

"I do not like liars. Why are you trembling?"

I did not want to say, "Because I think you are going to shoot me." I was afraid it would become fact. Once uttered, the words could not come back. They would reach their destination and spark the act. It was, is, a superstition of mine, an automatic reluctance to say what I fear most. There was always a chance it had not entered his mind, and I wasn't about to put it there.

"I... You might rape me or something." To me, this was so implausible, it had no chance of becoming reality. At twenty, I had never been on a date, never kissed. No boy had ever expressed an interest in me. I was not ugly, but I thought I was and carried myself accordingly. I was slightly plain and my habits were far enough outside what was considered normal, that I was never in a position to learn differently. I preferred study to parties, books to boyfriends. My knowledge of sex was limited to common cliches and finding ovaries in laboratory nematodes. Mama was distinctly old-fashioned and guarded such information as if it were a state secret.

I expected an answer along the lines of 'those with least to guard, guard it most fiercely'. I was prepared to be insulted by the man sitting before me and preferred an insult to a bullet. I was surprised, then, by his answer.

He regarded me silently for a moment before speaking. His blue eyes brushed over me, my frizzy hair, the glasses sliding down my nose, my baggy sweater and loose blue jeans.

"When I want sex," he said, "I prefer the woman to be willing. Are you willing?"

I could not answer at first. I did not know what he meant by this, but I was suddenly aware that there was a prospect worse than being shot by this man. It was the thought of being touched by him.

"No," I croaked.

"Do you have a boyfriend?"

"No."

"Ever had a boyfriend?"

"No."

He stood up and walked over to me. I dropped the paper bag as he grabbed the front of my jeans and unbuttoned them. I grasped frantically at his hand, trying to pull it away.

His other hand took the hair at the back of my head in a vise grip, pulled my head back, chin up. He kissed me then—if you can call it that. It was a violent, invasive, intimate investigation against my will. I was not accustomed to being helpless. It was an education. His right hand investigated, also roughly, with a savage precision that hurt more than my body.

He ended the kiss but kept his hold on me as he said. "Rape is not about sex. It is about power." He stared into my eyes; I barely saw him through my tears. "Do you need a lesson in power?"

"No," I sobbed.

He released me. I stood trembling in tears, grasping at my pants as if they were all I had (and they were, then).

"Now then," he said, "why are you shaking?"

"Because I am afraid you will shoot me."

"That is better. That is a reasonable answer. But I prefer to use a knife." He sat down again on the sofa. He spoke softly, in formal Russian. "I am more likely to cut your throat. Do you believe me, Alexandra Fyodorovna?"

"Yes."

"We are making progress. You are not Grayson's lover?"

"No!"

"And you do not work for him?"

"No."

"Who do you work for?"

"I've only ever had one job, at Sizzle Burger, but I don't think that is what you mean."

"Very good. Frank assures me that you are a typical American schoolgirl. I don't find you to be typical, and that bothers me. Stop shaking!"

I did my best, which was not very good. I stood, still stupidly holding my pants. He hadn't exactly done anything to put me at ease.

"I have taken into account your family background, but when you lie, it bothers me more."

"I haven't lied." As usual, my mouth ran off while my brain was occupied elsewhere, wondering what my family had to do with this.

He looked at me again and began to get up.

I corrected myself quickly. "Just the one time and my German is not that good."

He sat back down. "You conceal too much from me, Alexandra. Or you try to. It makes me wonder what you are up to."

Vasily opened a bottle of wine, poured some into a paper cup, and brought it to me. I was still holding my pants, unwilling to let them go. He put the cup down on the counter, gently pulled my hands away, and put me back together. I will never forget the look he gave me. It was not sympathetic or even compassionate, but a frank, knowing, look of regard. What Misha damaged, Vasily healed with one look. I loved him from that moment.

"What is in the bag?" he asked as he handed me the wine.

It was not the same wine as the night before, but it was nice and I took a long sip before I answered.

"Money."

"Money?"

"Money," I repeated. No one said a word. Nobody acted curious. Louis and Vasily set the coffee table with paper plates piled with coq au vin. They must have brought the ingredients with them. There certainly had been nothing more than cold pizza in my kitchen. The two men sat on the floor opposite Misha and all three began to eat. I stood there feeling ridiculous and hungry.

"Sit down," said Louis. "Eat." He pointed to a fourth plate on the little table.

I sat cautiously next to Misha and ate every scrap as if it were my last, a reasonable assumption given the circumstances. It was delicious. Louis is a wonderful cook.

It was Louis who finally asked about the money.

"So you carry your money in a sack?"

I looked at it. It was still on the floor where I dropped it, a few feet from the door.

"No. It isn't mine."

"Whose is it?"

"Yours?"

"Mine?"

"All of yours."

"All of ours?"

"I guess so. He said to give it to 'them,' and then he said to give it to Charlemagne, but I don't...." I realized my mistake when I saw the look on their faces.

"And who told you about Charlemagne?" asked Misha.

"Nobody." I struggled to gather my scrambled brain about me. "I mean, Grayson said it. I don't have any idea what it means."

"Somebody else said it, or you would not be so nervous."

"I'm nervous because you terrify me."

"Who else said it?" Misha persisted.

"Frank Cardova told me not to say it."

I still don't know how Misha reads me so accurately.

"He gave you good advice." Misha stood up. I shivered as he passed by me and picked up the bag. He looked inside it, then looked at me. "Charlemagne is our trade name. We," he gestured toward the other two, "are Charlemagne. Grayson told you to give this to us?"

"Yes."

"Why?"

"He said something about now that you have the money, you can go away."

"We want no money from him."

"I told him that."

Misha's puzzled expression narrowed. "And how did you know that?"

"Frank said it. He said something about it not being money."

"And you told Grayson that?"

"Yes."

"What did he say?"

"He said it didn't matter. That it should be enough to buy you off, and if you want more, he'll double it. There is fifty thousand dollars there, he said."

"Fifty thousand?"

All three men roared with laughter. I was not in on the joke. Not having ten dollars to spare, I did not find a bag of money particularly amusing. Misha threw the bag at me.

"Here," he said. "You keep it. Fifty thousand would not cover our expenses."

I knew I could not keep a bag full of cash of uncertain origin, but I was finally catching on and out of simple prudence did not argue with Misha.

Vasily was still chuckling. He sat on the floor, hands behind, legs stretched out before him. I tell you this because of what I saw in his laugh. I saw goodness. It lasted only a moment, but it was there, despite whatever other reality there might be, or that I would come to find out later, either in fact or in my imagination. There was a man there, who could laugh, not a monster.

We had coffee. Louis showed me how to pick a lock and gave me a few tools. Vasily and I discussed music. I thought his taste a little old-fashioned. I was beginning to relax when Misha sat next to me again.

He put one hand on my shoulder and turned me to face him. I feared the worst and tears started against my will. I bit my lip trying to hold them back.

"Stop that," he said. "I am not going to touch you."

I made an effort.

"We must make a decision about you." He said it rather gently—for Misha.

"If that's meant to make me feel better," I said, "it doesn't."

He ignored this and continued. "We live in a world with many secrets, Alex," he said. "Do you know that world?"

"No."

"Maybe not. You were born to it, but it seems, not brought up in it." He paused, watching me steadily. "We would like to meet your parents."

"My parents? Why?"

"Because then I will be sure you are what you say you are. Then I will know you are not working for Grayson or someone else. There have been too many coincidences that involve you. Is that plain enough?"

"Yes. But I don't see what my parents have to do with it."

"There is another reason." He paused and glanced over my shoulder at Vasily sitting behind me. "In our world, facts are very hard to determine. We can find anything in a file, but we rarely get the facts when something happens, because nobody will talk about it. Nobody. So we hear only rumors."

He paused, considering his next words. "We want to talk to your parents for two reasons: to make sure of who you are, and to clear up a rumor."

I did not point out that he was being as obtuse as any rumor maker. But I did finally stop shaking.

"The question," he continued, "is which one of us should go with you to meet them. I do not think we should all go."

That was a relief. I thought for a moment. Louis was the most charming and seemed relatively harmless, compared to the other two.

"Louis," I said.

Louis laughed, Vasily chuckled, and Misha smiled.

"Louis," said Misha as he suppressed a laugh, "is too dangerous."

I thought that was an odd statement coming from this man.

"He is very hot-headed," he explained, "and has no connection between his brain and his gun. I think I should go."

This was the last thing I wanted. "How about Vasily?" I asked.

"Vasily?" Misha rubbed his chin, then looked at Vasily. "Can you?"

"Yes."

"Are you sure?"

"Yes."

"Maybe you are right," he said to me. "It would be useless to have you next to me shaking all the time, and it is Vasily's business. Vasily will go in with you."

"Frank is here," said Louis.

I must mention here that Louis said this from the window. All three of them checked that window frequently. I don't think the street below was unobserved for more than a few seconds at a time. They also stopped talking whenever they heard my neighbors on the stairs. At times I fancied they acted more like the hunted than the hunters.

"I've been looking all over for you guys," said Frank when he came in.

"Then you are pretty stupid," said Misha.

"I love it when you flatter me, and it's nice to see the girl still in one piece. How are you doing, Alex?"

"Fine. Thank you." It wasn't a lie, but I have felt better.

"Fine? Good. Are we all through here? Satisfied? Ready to get on with it and leave the girl alone?" He emphasized 'alone'.

"Not quite," said Misha.

"What now?"

"Vasily is going to meet her parents."

"He is?" There was a note of panic in Frank's voice. "That's not safe, in my judgment."

"You have no judgment, Frank."

"Let's not be hasty. Tell you what; why don't I nip downtown and pull the file? I know I can get you authorization to read it."

"Your files mean nothing, Frank."

"But they are informative."

"Vasily will learn more this way."

"But let me have a minute with Alex, will you?"

"No. If you have anything to say to her, say it here."

Frank looked at me, biting his lower lip. He glanced at Vasily, then back at me. "Tell your Dad," he said, "that Buddy says Hi. Tell him I'm on the all-star team now."

FOURTEEN

I led a simple life then. For example, going from one place to another posed problems only when the distance required a form of transportation I could not afford. When this was the case, I stayed put. I was never vexed with the paradox of Zeno. It did not bother me that I could never, logically, travel distance A because this would require me to first travel one half of A, then one half of the one half, and so on, ad infinitum, never starting out or ending up. When I was twenty and wanted to go somewhere, I either stayed put or I went. It was that simple.

Not so with Charlemagne. My parents lived three miles away. The discussion required to cover it took half an hour. First, should we take my new car or the Mercedes? I wondered how we would take the Mercedes when that was chosen because I had not seen it parked outside. Next came a conversation, no, a plan—yes, it was a carefully laid plan—of how we would leave the building, what route we would take to the car, and who would watch our backs.

Today, this procedure is second nature to me; then, I thought it silly. They took it seriously, though.

The Mercedes was parked on another street half a block away. Vasily and I made our way to it. I say 'made our way' and not walked because what we did to get there cannot be construed as walking. Skulking might be a better word, but still not entirely accurate. Skulking in an apparently natural way? Maybe. At any rate, we stayed in shadows, often with a wall on one side. Vasily seemed to prefer this and stopped frequently to listen.

At the car, he produced a small, powerful flashlight and inspected the Mercedes before he touched it. He looked underneath it and in the wheel wells. Satisfied, he unlocked the front passenger door and searched the interior, under the seats and the dashboard. This took only a few moments, but he was so careful and so serious it frightened me.

"Is this car more like me?" he asked when we were safely on our way.

"Yes and no," I said. "It's not a girl's car, but it's not you, either."

"Do you like your new car?" he asked. "Does it suit you?"

"I like it very much. Thank you. But it doesn't fit me."

"Nothing fits for you tonight, does it?"

"I guess not."

"Why doesn't the car fit you?"

"It's too pretty. I'm more the old Volkswagen type."

He paused for a moment, then said with what sounded like anger, "Alex, you are not ugly. Stop talking that way. Stop thinking that way. It is not humility; it is foolishness, and it causes you problems in other areas, like sex. That was an incredibly stupid thing to say to Misha. You are hopelessly naive in some respects."

I was still working on 'You are not ugly'. Besides Papa, no man had ever said that to me. This was new. This was a revelation. "Are you saying I'm pretty?" I asked, incredulous.

"A woman need not be pretty to be attractive, Alex."

"I'm not pretty."

"No. But you are not ugly."

"Plain, then."

"No. Definitely attractive."

How can I describe how those two words affected me, especially to you, a young woman who has never doubted her own extraordinary beauty?

I changed the subject so his compliment could not be changed, expanded, or depleted by further explanation. "Why do you take such pains to look inconspicuous," I asked, "and yet drive a distinctive car?"

"It is not distinctive in the places where we usually drive it," said Vasily. "We have this car for three reasons. Frank gave it to us; it is equipped with everything we need, and Misha likes it."

That made sense. "Misha likes things to be elegant and beautiful, doesn't he?"

"Don't insult yourself again."

"I'm not. I just get the impression Misha doesn't like me."

"You are insignificant to him. That is all."

"Who is significant?"

"His friends and his enemies."

"Who are his friends?"

"Louis, me, his family."

"He has a family?"

"Yes."

"A wife?"

"Yes. Stop acting surprised and do not say a word of this to Frank."

I could not help acting surprised. I could not imagine any of these men married. Another thought gave me a sudden pain. I approached the subject cautiously.

"Does Louis?"

"Does Louis what?"

"Does Louis have a wife?"

"No."

I could not ask. There was a long pause, during which we pulled up in front of my parents' house. Vasily turned off the engine.

"Neither do I," he said, "but in a few minutes, I think, that will not matter to you."

FIFTEEN

Mama answered the door.

"Mama, may I introduce Vasily Sobieski?"

She did not move but stood frozen in place looking at him steadily. "I carried you out." She spoke Russian.

"Yes. I remember."

"You were four years old."

Papa called from another room.

Mama stepped aside and ushered us in. "It's Alex, Fyodor," she called. "She has brought... someone."

She looked again at Vasily. "You've grown tall and good-looking." She seemed to debate her next comment before saying it. "You favor your father—in looks."

"Yes," he said. "I favor my father."

"I brought you to an Austrian family. That was your mother's instruction. A well-to-do family. They had a son a year or two older, and a Polish housekeeper. Michael, I think they called him. The boy, I mean. Did you get on well?"

"We grew up like brothers."

"Good. Good. Please, sit down."

"No, thank you. I will stand."

He stood with his back to the fireplace, hands in his pockets. Papa's chair was in the corner on his right, another chair, the one my mother had indicated when inviting him to sit, was on his left, the front door behind it. In front of him was the sofa, where I sat down next to Mama, my jaw still dragging the floor. Behind me, a single hallway led to all the other rooms in the house. There had once been a separate entrance to the kitchen to the right of Papa's chair, but my father had closed it up. Having too many doors was only appropriate in certain buildings, he said, not in his home.

Papa came in from the hallway, paused, then sat in his chair.

"Please," he said to Vasily, "sit down."

Vasily stayed where he was.

"Papa," I said, "this is…"

"Yes, I know, Alex."

"Papa, I'm to tell you Buddy said 'Hi,' and…."

"Buddy?" He looked at Vasily, his jaw clenched. "Still your babysitter?"

"We know him as Frank," said Vasily.

"We? Are you still together then? Where are the others?"

"Elsewhere."

"You must be uncomfortable." Papa put his hand to his forehead. "Of course. My apologies. Here, take my seat. I'm well out of it; I'll sit with my back to the door." He got up and sat in the other chair.

Vasily sat in Papa's chair.

Papa turned to me and said, "You know Alex, there are some animals that cannot sleep unless they are touching a secure surface. These guys are like that."

I was still processing my mother's words and did not know what he meant. But he was about to tell me.

"I hear you're major league now," Papa said to Vasily. "Is that true?"

"I am not acquainted with American jargon," Vasily answered.

Frank's words seemed to fit here, so I interrupted. "Frank said to tell you he's on the all-star team."

My father's eyebrows arched. "Charlemagne is number one now, is it? Where's the team captain, the one with the knife?"

Vasily did not answer.

"And the wiz kid, the Frenchman? Listening in, I imagine." Papa stretched his neck and leaned over each side of the chair as if looking for something.

"I thought you said you were well out of it?" said Vasily.

"I keep up with the news. I assigned Frank to you guys, you know. Long ago, when you were trigger-happy brats and Frank showed some potential. I understand you're quite a weapons man. It fits, given your history. Next question is, what are you doing with my daughter?"

"We are not sure about her."

"Frank told you she's clear, surely."

"His information is not always accurate."

"It's as accurate as it gets."

"People are more informative than files."

Papa scratched his chin. "Whatever this is, it must be big, and it's going wrong."

"Yes."

"And my daughter?"

"She turns up every time it goes wrong."

"Well, I assure you, she's not in the game. Where is Frank, by the way? With the other two? What's he think he's doing?"

"He thinks he is doing his best."

"His best to stay alive, I imagine. Is my daughter the only reason you're here?"

"No."

"I thought not. Your father?"

There was a pause before Vasily answered, in a low, flat voice, staring at the carpet in front of him. "I was told he was shot with his own gun."

I looked at his face, wondering what was going on, what on earth these people, people I thought I knew, were talking about. Vasily looked up. His grey eyes held no expression, no emotion at all. They were two-way mirrors. He could look out, but I could see nothing inside. My parents had suddenly arrived from another planet.

"Don't look at me!" said Papa. "I was just his babysitter. I never touched his gun."

"What's a babysitter, Papa?" I was tired of ignorance.

"A babysitter controls a specialist, Alex. He provides the logistics support he needs: cars, safehouses, papers, that sort of thing, helps locate and isolate the target, and," with a pointed look at Vasily, "keeps him from contaminating the local populace. Something Frank's not managing too well."

Vasily shrugged. "There has been a question as to whether your daughter qualifies as a member of the local populace."

"That's all we have ever wanted her to be," said Mama. She leaned forward when she said this, treating Vasily to one of her more malevolent gazes.

"She has picked up some traits then, despite your efforts."

"Yes. Despite our best efforts."

I interrupted again quickly. "I have a right to know what's going on now, Papa. Tell me what a specialist is."

"You have no such right, young lady," said Papa. "But I suppose sometimes the lack of information can be as dangerous as the possession of it. Maybe you need to know."

He looked at Vasily briefly. Vasily was looking at the floor again, but he raised his clear eyes and watched my face as Papa explained.

"A specialist is someone who does what has to be done when no one else will do it. He hunts terrorists and solves strategic problems. Other words? Hunter. Killer. Assassin. Most of them work roughly along ideological lines, but they belong to no government. They are for hire."

Somehow, I had suspected this, but the spoken word hurt. I could not look at Vasily. I studied my hands in my lap as my father continued.

"Your friend here is the explosives expert for the best specialist team in the world. Their success record is one hundred percent. Never beaten."

I was beginning to cry, but Papa was not finished.

"The reason they are so successful is because they are very smart, very skilled, and ruthless. That is why Buddy is their babysitter. He is the best we have and it takes the best to keep such a weapon from exploding in our faces."

My tears were not entirely for Vasily. My father's involvement was an alien idea to me, though I finally understood some of his eccentricities.

"We?" I asked. "Do you mean the government? You weren't—Frank isn't—one of them?"

"No. I was not a specialist. I worked for Uncle Sam. But don't take relief from that, Alex. In any world where responsibility is understood and taken seriously, there are no grades of guilt, only levels of skill."

"Uncle Sam? But you were Russian."

"No, I wasn't."

"You were born in Leningrad."

"No. Cincinnati."

Vasily interrupted. "We are wasting time," he said impatiently. "Will you tell me about my father, or not?"

Papa did not answer him. He turned to me instead. I felt rather than saw Vasily's exasperation. I still could not bring myself to look at him.

"Alex," said Papa. "A specialist's greatest nightmare is to die by his own gun. It means treachery, betrayal. Usually, only one other person has access to it. Usually, that is his lover. A team is slightly different since they all have access—as do all their lovers. They take a bigger risk in treachery, but they have greater safety with someone to cover their backs, so they can sleep. Do you see?"

I saw, but I did not know why he was telling me this.

He turned to Vasily. "Your father was an ace. Only one person had access."

Mama spoke then, gently, so gently that I had to look at her to make sure it was her speaking. She spoke in Russian. "There was no choice," she said. "You were directly threatened. It was your father or you."

I finally managed a glance at Vasily. He sat like a stone.

"And my mother?"

"They took her before they knew he was dead," said Mama. "They knew who she was, knew she had access. You were on your way to Austria when she died."

She turned to me. "Help me make coffee, Alex."

I did not want to go, but the signals from both my parents were unmistakable and imperative. In the kitchen, I could hear the murmur of the two men in the other room. I wanted to listen, but Mama planted herself in front of me, took both my shoulders in her hands, and said, "Listen. That man in there, is he anything to you?"

I did not know what to say. Indeed, I did not know what to feel.

"If he is or if he isn't, I will tell you anyway. I saw his father dead, Alex, but more important, I saw him before he was dead, and he was already a corpse. Do you understand me, Alex? He was already a corpse, his soul murdered bit by bit with every killing. He was an animal; no human lived in that body. He was a collection of finely honed reflexes, nothing more. That man in there," she pointed to the living room, "is the same. He is empty. He is a corpse."

"All men can change, Mama. You have said it many times."

"No. Not this man. You don't understand. Even if he did turn, his enemies would kill him immediately. Don't you see? For him to quit, to really quit, he has to stop defending himself. He is hunted. He is always under attack. To stop means death, for him and anyone close to him. I give him five days, no more. Don't think you can do it, Alex. It is more likely he would turn you, make an animal of you. You are too young."

"But I am strong, Mama."

"You think you are."

"We must face all our choices with courage. You detest cowards, especially moral cowards, as much as I do."

"Yes, but there is a difference between a hero and a fool."

We made coffee and brought a tray to the living room, but Vasily was standing, ready to leave.

"Alex can stay here tonight," said Papa. "I will take her home in the morning."

Vasily looked at me. "I will take you home now," he said.

"It's no trouble," said my father. "I will take her."

Vasily's gaze was steady. I could not read it. "It is your choice, Alex," he said quietly.

I went home with Vasily.

SIXTEEN

We drove to my flat in silence. Vasily seemed preoccupied. So was I.

Frank, Louis, and Misha were waiting downstairs. Misha opened my car door. "Well?" he said to Vasily.

"She is clear."

"She had better stay that way."

Vasily did not answer. Misha addressed me. "I will walk upstairs with you."

"Please, don't bother."

"I'll walk her up," said Frank. He shifted on his feet from side to side, as if preparing to run. I knew he would not run. He was just nervous.

They had a discussion. Frank said he needed my signature on a form. Misha was impatient, with Frank—and me.

"Give me the paper," he said and grabbed it from Frank's hand. He pulled me out of the car and pushed me up the stairs in front of him, ushering me into my apartment in a hurry.

"I hope you are not so stupid that I must tell you to be discreet," he said.

"I'm not stupid." I was shaking again, but more from anger than fear. "And I don't like you at all."

He almost smiled. "Why don't you like me, Alex?"

"You are evil."

"I suppose you are a saint?"

"No. But at least I don't kill people."

"The difference between us, Alex, is not that I kill and you do not. It is that death surrounds me; it only puzzles you."

I scrunched up my eyebrows at him, confused, and he explained.

"When death is no longer only an idea in your philosophical little head, when you see it and smell it and are faced with only evil alternatives regarding it, perhaps you will have a claim to moral superiority. But I doubt it. Until then, I advise you to hate me less intensely, because hate is the next thing to murder and murder is not appropriate in an aspiring saint. Now sign this for Frank." He put the form on the counter and handed me a pen.

"What does it say?" I asked.

"Your government is informing you that if you say anything, the best thing that will happen to you is that you will go to jail."

"It says that?"

"It says some of that. I say the rest."

I understood him perfectly but took my time reading it anyway. I wanted to irritate him. He snatched the forms and pen from me as soon as I signed and let himself out without another word.

Good riddance.

...

Midnight is an odd time to run errands, I admit, but it was the best time for me—some things must be done without witnesses. After a check of the surrounding streets, I drove to the church and used Louis's tools to open the door. He had taught me well. I had no trouble. I quickly finished the two things I wanted to do and went home knowing the bag of money was safe but accessible.

...

I spent the next day expecting to see Vasily. I attended all my classes, a rare enough event, but it did me little good. My mind was on the cars driving by, looking for a black Mercedes. I concentrated on the people in the hallways, not my books, looking for a sandy-haired man of medium height with a solemn demeanor and a hint of exceptional strength. I was disappointed. I told myself I was being silly. I tried to convince myself that this was a foolish preoccupation with a man I was better off without.

When my last class ended, I avoided the narrow walkway I took the day before. I wanted no more surprises. I stayed on a well-lit path that wound around the biology building and was about midway down the walk when I heard steps running behind me. As I turned to see who it was, something hit me squarely in the chest and sent me sprawling backward to the ground, my books scattered under a path light. That light was my only company, and it did me precious little good.

"You think you're something," my attacker said. "I'll show you something."

Boris was on top of me, grabbing at my skirt, pulling it up, and tearing at my pantyhose. I struggled with everything in me. I fought him with a fury I never felt before. It was a question of power, all right, a struggle for power that I had to win. He was determined to show me and I was equally determined to prevent him.

I was winning until he cheated. He pulled out a knife and held it to my face, then moved it to my throat. I could see the bruise under his eye where I had hit him. I saw weakness and malice in his fleshy, unshaven face and I hated him intensely.

"I'll cut you," he said through his teeth.

"Cut her, and I cut you." It was a foreign voice, and it came at the same moment another knife flashed between our faces, razor edge toward Boris.

"Drop your knife and get up," said Misha's voice. I recognized it and was glad the edge of his knife faced away from me.

Boris got up and dropped his knife.

Louis pulled me up, helped to smooth my skirt, and brushed the dust from my clothes and hair. I saw Misha standing in the light, the point of that knife under Boris's chin. Boris babbled, hands raised, chin as high as he could hold it. Vasily stood to one side.

Louis led me away and Misha put the knife away and walked toward us. He walked on my left, Louis on my right. I heard Boris mumble something, then a dull thud. I turned to see where Vasily was, but Louis put his arm around my shoulder and led me firmly away.

"He won't kill him, will he?" I asked, not really wanting an answer.

"No," said Louis. "Nick will live."

We crossed a grassy area in the science quadrangle. The campus was emptying after the last class of the day. A steadily diminishing stream of cars left the surrounding parking lots. We sat on a bench and waited.

"I thought you didn't speak English," I said to Misha after a few minutes.

"I understand enough to know that is not a gracious thank you."

"Where is Vasily?" I asked.

He did not answer. We were silent for another minute until Vasily joined us. We walked to the parking lot, Misha and Louis in front, Vasily and I lagging behind.

"About Saturday," he said, "I will not be here and must break our date."

"Oh." I tried to act unconcerned. "Everything is going all right now?"

"No. It is still not right, but we should finish tomorrow and be gone quickly." He stopped, took my arm, and turned me to face him. "I never had any intention of being here on Saturday."

I waited for him to finish, not wanting him to say anything. I wanted him to leave now so I could cry privately.

"But I would like to have dinner with you," he said. "Without Misha there to make you tremble, eh?"

He smiled and Humpty Dumpty was put back together.

"Yes."

"It may be some time before I can come back. Your government does not often welcome me. Will you have dinner with me when I come back?"

I nodded, and he kissed me. It was my first kiss. (I do not count the incident with Misha as a kiss for obvious reasons.) To dinner? I would have gone to Mars with him. What I knew about him, what he was, what he was about to do, what he could have done, disappeared in the joy of holding him and of being held by him. There were no other considerations, no other facts. There was only his kiss, his touch, and it was enough for me.

The Mercedes was already behind my car when we reached the parking lot. Vasily watched as I started it before he joined the others. Then the Mercedes turned onto the street, pulled over briefly for a passing ambulance, and left the campus, and me, for what I thought would be too long a time.

I settled down to wait for him, though, and spent the next day in a dream world of first love, attributing everything noble to my lover, blaming every nagging reminder of reality on the evil influence of Misha, and supplying the required miracle of righteous change in Vasily from my fertile imagination.

That evening, the evening of the day after my first kiss, at about six, my comfortable dream world of gentle miracles turned into a nightmare. In one of my nightmares, I am most terrified not by what happens to me, but by the part I play in it. If I am attacked in my dream, my inability to scream is what makes it a nightmare. If I fall from a great height, it is the last step I take before the fall that is most disturbing, because it is most regretted.

I was aglow with virtue and good intentions as I made a frugal supper in my tiny kitchen after school that evening. There was a knock at the door; it was Father Paul. In retrospect, I find it appropriate that it was a priest who broke my pious reverie and introduced me to a night of hell.

SEVENTEEN

"Are you busy?" Father Paul asked when I opened the door.

"No, Father, why?"

"Can you come with me? To the hospital? Boris Nikitin is very bad. He may die."

I remembered a voice from distant yesterday saying "Nick will live."

I shuddered.

"He wants to see you," continued the priest.

"Me? Why?"

"He won't say. But he desperately wants to see you. Can you come?"

I followed him to the hospital in my car because Father Paul was determined to stay with Boris until he was out of danger. Danger? When we arrived at the hospital, he told me he would wait outside the room.

"He's very bad," he said. "Don't stay too long."

I stood inside the door for a moment, staring at the thing before me. All my early virtue disappeared in the face of this reality I could not deny. The man I loathed was no longer a man; he was a pulp. The man I loved had never been a man. Only an animal could have done this. I could not pass this off conveniently to the evil Misha; he had been in my sight the whole time. Vasily had done this, was the only one who could have done this. He did this without apparent effort, certainly without compunction, and then he kissed me.

Boris was difficult to pick out in the jungle of tubes and bandages. Every limb was encased in plaster.

His hands, suspended from a frame above him, were double their normal size with fingers spread by silver splints. His face, a blot of purple and red surrounded by hospital white, was swollen and unrecognizable. His nose was broken, his jaw wired together. He looked at me through one blood-filled eye; the other had been forced shut by the swelling.

I went to his side. He murmured something.

I bent closer to hear him.

"Forgive me," he said.

I don't know how long I knelt by that bed crying. It was a space of time outside of time. It ended when Father Paul came into the room.

"They think he will make it," he said gently. "Why don't you go home now, Alex?"

...

A mountain of stairs faced me at my apartment building. I climbed it one boulder at a time, watching my feet, and so I did not see Brent Grayson waiting on the landing by my door until it was too late. He grabbed me by my sweater and slammed me against the door, pushing the muzzle of a gun into my face so hard that it cut the inside of my cheek on a tooth.

"I'm going to die and you're going with me," he said.

I had no time to answer him. He was sweating, taut, heated by desperate fear, talking fast and without coherence.

"You didn't give it to them," he said.

"I did," I insisted, searching the stairwell for an escape.

"They're on me. They're dogging me. What did they say?"

"They laughed," I said with difficulty.

His color changed; he turned scarlet, convulsed with rage, fierce, and out of control. He hissed, "Laughed? Open your mouth so I can shoot you in your laughing throat."

I caught sight of a movement to my left, behind Grayson's shoulder. It was Louis. He held a finger to his lips in a gesture of silence. His other hand held a gun. He took aim.

"Open!" said Grayson.

"Wait," I said in desperation. "I know where the icon is."

He paused. There came a sharp pop from Louis's suppressed gun and Grayson was dead, slumping against me, then crumpling to the floor.

Louis was putting his gun away when Misha came up the stairs, two at a time.

"What the hell!" he said. "Open the door. Get that inside before someone comes along."

Louis had the door open before I could find my key. Vasily came upstairs and helped Misha pull the body inside. They put it in the bathtub. Louis escorted me in and bolted the door behind us all. The body did not frighten me as much as the wild look on Misha's face. It was a fury very much like Grayson's had been, but more controlled and therefore, to me, more surely deadly. He and Louis held a heated discussion in French that I did not understand.

Louis's temper flared. I was trying to edge away from the two of them when Louis said suddenly, in English, "She knows the location of the icon."

I did not like the attention I received then. Misha's gaze made the bones inside me sizzle. He said, "You know where the icon is?"

"Yes."

"Where?"

I was about to answer when Vasily said something in Polish. Another long and incomprehensible discussion followed. Vasily spoke quietly; Misha was more vehement. I did not speak Polish at the time, so I do not know exactly what was said, but Vasily told me later that it was an argument over my right to a free choice. He said I was the eventual loser, depending on one's point of view, but he never told me which way he argued.

Eventually, they decided something, because there came a flurry of questions. What was my dress size? Shoe size? Was there a store open? Where were my car keys? Louis and Vasily left, and I was alone in my apartment with Misha and a dead body.

Misha bolted the door, then went to the window. The curtains were closed and he stood by the far-right side of the window looking out through the narrow space where the curtain did not cover the side. He looked around the room and pulled the sofa away from the wall and slightly toward him. The side of the sofa was low, about two feet high. He rested one foot on it, leaned against the wall, and checked the street behind the curtain again.

I recognized it and remembered doing something similar—an alarm made from pots and pans. "You're afraid," I said to him, amazed.

He looked at me and I noticed other things. He was unshaven, his hair uncombed, his eyes puffy. He was tired.

"This place is not safe," he said. "Come here, so I can talk to you."

I approached warily.

"Ten days ago," he said, "we arrived to do a job that should take only two days. Everything was ready; then something went wrong. For ten days we have been living with only the protection Frank can give, and it is not enough.

The entire black world knows we are here and exposed; our enemies are ready to exploit it. We are making too many mistakes."

"And you're afraid of dying," I said.

"No. Dying is nothing. Louis did Grayson a great favor by putting a bullet in his head. Much worse awaited him."

"Then why not quit now?"

"I don't know. Maybe you will tell me the answer to that tomorrow."

I wondered what he meant by this.

"Please describe the icon and tell me where it is." I told him, and he asked, "Then it can be taken apart? Into sections?"

"I suppose it can, but it is ancient. I am not sure it can be dismantled without damage."

"We will go get it. But first I will explain something to you. Sometimes people make choices for us, but even then, we can—we must—accept or reject the choice. That is unavoidable. Even by not choosing, we choose. Do you understand?"

"No."

"You will."

EIGHTEEN

W e drove past the church and parked on an unlighted side street. Misha opened the fire exit door in the back and we slipped inside.

The moonlight glinted in sparks on the gold, on the candles, and on the icons. The iconostasis guarded the holiest place and hid the altar from our view, but the saints were here, in profusion, as witnesses. The prayers, of joy, despair—and sometimes boredom—clung to the walls, lingered under the ceiling, assaulted the senses in the same way the incense did, reminding out and breathing in devotion to God.

I knew the saints were furious with me for bringing this man into that holy place. I asked them to please pray for me anyway.

We crossed behind the icon of Saint Sergius—oh, the look he must have given me at the sight of my companion!—and entered a little room to one side of the main entrance. The room, a closet really, was barely large enough to hold the two of us. Opposite the door, a tall cupboard took up one

wall. It was filled with hanging vestments and boxes of candles. A sink and short counter stood against the wall on our
left. There were no windows. Misha shut the door and
turned on the light.

He stood above me as I knelt in front of the sink cabinet,
searching for the opening I knew was there. I dug my fingers
into the carpet, under the cabinet's baseboard. It pulled away
easily. I reached in and slid the folded icon out from under
the cabinet. Misha knelt beside me, regarding me curiously,
as if he hadn't expected me to produce the icon.

"How did you find it?" he asked. "Did you hide it?"

"No. I just knew where to start looking."

"How?"

"Cleaning supplies. They're in the cabinet."

"Please, explain."

I tried to keep it simple. "The person who cleans the
church hid the icon. It was logical for her to hide it in a place
she knows well."

He was still puzzled, so I started from the beginning.

"Father Paul was about to sell the icon to Grayson, but
something happened, and he backed out of the deal at the
last minute. That night, the icon disappeared. Grayson
wanted it badly, but he didn't have it. Boris was there because he was watching Grayson for Vasily. He didn't know
anything about it, and anyway, there was no sign of forced
entry. Boris would have broken a window or something. Not
his style to forego malicious damage. Vasily didn't have it

because he kept asking me about it. That eliminates just about everybody who doesn't have a key.

"That brought me to a dead end until Papa taught me something the night he met Vasily. It was the concept of access. One other person had access to the key. One person who knew about the proposed sale and knew the reason it fell through. One person who would have heard everything Father Paul told the bishop's secretary behind a useless dining room partition. That was Erin, the Matushka."

"She took the icon to sell it against her husband's wishes," said Misha.

"No." I looked at him, hoping he would understand what I was about to tell him. "It may have occurred to her to sell the icon. She even called Grayson. When I went to see him, he thought I was her. That's why he was so quick to let me in and that's how I knew he didn't have the icon. But somehow, she must have decided against it and told him it was missing. When I came, he thought she had found it and changed her mind. But Erin would not have sold it, because as much as they need the money, that wasn't why she hid it."

"Why, then?"

"Because of the miracle."

His eyebrows went up, waiting for an explanation. I told him about Mara, and about the laughter Father Paul had heard. "Erin didn't take the icon to sell it. She took it to protect her husband from being called a fool."

"Do you mean there was no miracle?" he asked.

I could not tell if he was skeptical, or simply studying me, my words, and my expression. He was attentive, for sure.

"It doesn't matter if there was or was not a miracle," I said. "Don't you see?"

He shook his head.

I tried again. "Erin grew up in the western church. Her view is Western, and practical, based on the material, the visible, and the scientific. Miracles are explainable. They may be miracles, but there is always a natural explanation. Mara's, and then Father Paul's, miracle could not be explained. Erin did not believe it and was afraid it would open her otherwise sensible husband to ridicule and criticism. She couldn't bear this. She hid the icon. It was too big and awkward to move it far, and indeed, she didn't want to move it far. She only wanted it out of the way for a little while until her husband came to his senses."

"So was there a miracle?"

I remember his question so clearly, his insistence on an answer. I wonder now what answer he wanted.

I said, "I agree with Erin that Father Paul is too sensible to imagine such a thing. Mara, maybe, but Father Paul? Also, I'm an American, so my thinking is essentially Western. Unlike Erin, though, my heritage is Eastern. Some things need not be explained. Some things just are." I kept my eyes on the icon and continued in a whisper. "I believe there was a miracle."

I looked up to see Misha staring at me intently. He broke his gaze, took out his knife, and began prying a hinge off of one of the smaller panels. When the panel had been removed, he pushed the rest of the icon back under the sink and replaced the baseboard.

I held the icon panel on my lap as we drove back to the apartment. Misha asked me questions as we traveled, about many things, but said only one thing I found illuminating.

"Vasily is anxious that you should live."

NINETEEN

V asily and Louis were waiting at my apartment. They had several packages of new clothing and were busy cutting the tags out of each piece, using razor-sharp knives that were not pocket knives. Louis's knife had a serrated edge. A pile of black clothing lay on the floor against the wall under the window.

The new clothing—the stuff they were sanitizing—was feminine. This bothered me because I expected them to leave now that they had the icon or part of it. I hoped they would take the body in the bathtub with them and I was ready to say goodbye. But Louis was undeniably holding a skirt, a short, aqua, jersey knit that I was sure could not possibly be for me.

"So long, then," I said, deciding on a direct approach.

"We are not leaving," said Louis.

"Yes, you are. You have the icon. Now go."

Misha leaned the icon against the wall and sat down on the sofa. "Come here, Alex," he said.

I went toward him, but not too close. He pointed to the coffee table in front of the sofa. "Sit down."

I sat on the table facing him. He looked at me for a long time before he began. He made me feel as if we were the only two people in the room. He had my attention.

"You must help us," he began.

"I can't possibly help you."

"You can, and you must. I will explain." He leaned forward. "There are two brothers. They are a team, like us, but they are not as skilled as we are, and they do not command the best prices. They have begun descending into terrorism for attention. And they are the worst of terrorists because they are indiscriminate. Do you remember the Paris metro bombing?"

"Yes."

"That was their work. Their trade name is Ill Wind. We call them Achim and Ahmed, for want of a better name."

I must have looked puzzled because he stopped and took more time to explain.

"We use trade names because other names are not permanent; they change with the identities we use. Some of us, like Vasily, have an advantage in people knowing our real names. His advantage comes from his father. But otherwise, we have no real names, except in police files or Interpol. So you see, it is pointless to tell you the real names of Achim and Ahmed. Those are the names they used with Grayson this time, their game names for this operation.

"I also cannot tell you what their alliance is, only that they kill. They use one cause after another as a cover for their demonstrations, but their purpose is to show what they are capable of and to advertise their skill. But they are too unstable and no one will hire or supply them. Several governments, yours included, have decided it is time for them to go, and we have the commission. It is a very large commission because no one else can or will take the risk."

"This is far beyond me," I said. "I'm just a college kid." I whispered this last because I was mesmerized by him and by his words. It was like an initiation, and I suspected that it was more than he had said on this subject for a long time, because he paused frequently, as if to form sentences around ideas that were not commonly spoken.

"I am getting to your place in this," he said. "Ill Wind is planning another operation. They will use the last of their explosive. But it is a very delicate operation and they need the newest technology to achieve it. They need a laser detonation system. Normally, no one will sell it to them, but one typically irresponsible government has agreed to give the system (which they stole from the Americans) to Ill Wind in return for something their prime minister can present in Moscow on a state visit next month. They hope to impress the Soviets with an important acquisition. Besides pleasing Moscow, they want to sink a hook into Ill Wind. There is always more than one motive, more than one plan, in any move of this game."

He shifted in his seat and sighed as if despairing of my ever catching on. I must have looked pretty unintelligent. I felt it. He leaned forward again, held me fast in that bright blue gaze, and continued.

"The hook was to be the icon. The plan was to blow up the Sears Tower. Completely. That was ten days ago. Achim and Ahmed arrived, with us on their heels. They met Grayson and he agreed to produce the icon. I do not know what his plan was, but he was desperate for money and I do not think he ever intended to pay your priest. But that is not important now. He was supposed to bring the icon, and Ill Wind would then trade it for the system. They would wire the building and make a very loud noise. Everything was supposed to be finished in twenty-four hours. But something went wrong. There was no icon.

"The brothers are well protected. We cannot get at them until they move. They will not move until they get the detonators. They cannot get the detonators until they have the icon. Do you see where I am leading?"

"Yes," I said.

"You have the icon."

"But now you have it. You can give it to them."

He smiled slightly, as much of a smile as one is likely to see on Misha. "They are prepared only for Grayson to give it to them," he said. "Tonight was to be his last chance to produce it. Now he is dead." He gave a side glance to Louis. "For a day or two we thought you worked for Grayson. Maybe they will think so, too."

"Maybe?" I did not like the sound of this.

"Listen carefully." He gave me a set of instructions, specific and simple. There were several important things that I had to remember, one of which was to forget everything he had just told me. I was more than willing to do that.

What is interesting, as I look back on it, is that he never asked me if I was willing to help in the first place. He assumed, and I never objected. I never thought to object to being an accomplice to a killing; I thought only about preventing another tragedy. I was part of a decision on who should die, but not in an affirmative way. My involvement was based on my circumstances, on the influence of the powerful man who sat opposite me, and on my own moral ambiguities. My subsequent actions were not heroic because I never decided. I never chose either side or no side.

But that absolves me of nothing. The *no* option was always open and I knew that. It would have meant death, but it was open all the same. Morality was a maze I could not negotiate. I did as I was told because I was not mentally prepared to object.

There was another area, though, where my moral training was explicit and indelible and we quickly came to it.

TWENTY

"Take off your clothes," said Misha.

"What?" I was horrified.

"You must wear these." He pointed to the aqua skirt and accessories.

"Take off your clothes."

I stood before him now, shaking. I took off my jeans.

"The sweater. Hurry up," he said.

I complied.

He produced his knife and walked behind me as I stood trembling in my underwear. He tugged at my panties, cutting out the tag at the back. He stood in front of me again, reached behind, and slipped his fingers under the bottom elastic of my bra. He was looking for another tag, but it was too much for me. I broke down with a sob and pulled away.

"*Scheisse!*" He pulled me back by the arm, searched again roughly for the tag, found it, and cut it. "She is useless," he said to Vasily as he released me. "She will never survive. Look at her." Then he shouted at me, "Stop it!"

He was frightful. I shivered and sobbed. Louis handed me a checkered sweatshirt that matched the aqua skirt. I put it on quickly, anxious to put anything I could between me and all that venom.

Misha pointed at Vasily. "You must fix it," he said. "She cannot face Achim like this. He will know everything in five minutes."

Vasily crossed the room to where I stood half-dressed and miserable, put his arm around my shoulder, and led me to the sofa where we sat down together.

"Alex," he said gently, "please, listen to me."

My heart poured out gratitude with my tears. But my adoring look disturbed him. He looked away, then at Misha. I could not help but follow his eyes to Misha's grim, uncompromising face. When Vasily turned back to me, his expression had hardened; it was no longer gentle. I felt isolated again but made more of an effort to control the tears.

"Understand," said Vasily, "the operation comes first. Many lives depend on it, including ours, and you will not be allowed to jeopardize it."

I nodded. I understood.

"You are necessary to the operation because Ill Wind is not going to accept the icon from anyone else. We are not sure they will accept it from you. Their deal is with Grayson. If there is a variation, it must be logical."

He shifted uncomfortably, then spoke again without looking at me. He looked at my hands, in his hands. "There are always at least two ways to proceed in any situation. In this case, you can hand over the icon at once, be questioned briefly or not at all, and then shot, or you can hand over only part of the icon and be questioned at length."

Here was new information. I began to listen carefully. The word 'shot' was especially illuminating, and I wondered how many other revelations lurked in Vasily's next words. I lost the tears in a rush of fear.

"There are arguments for and against both plans."

Mind if I add some of my own arguments? May I please state my druthers concerning the prospects of being shot? And could I have a precise definition of 'questioned'?

I was about to get that definition.

"It has been agreed that you should take only a part of the icon. It is a better plan operationally."

At this, Misha gave an exasperated sigh.

"It is," insisted Vasily.

"Yes, yes, sure," said Misha holding us his hands up in surrender.

"It is better operationally and it will give you a chance of survival," Vasily told me.

"So what does 'questioned at length' mean?" I asked.

Vasily's brow wrinkled, shading his colorless eyes.

"You said if I brought them only part of the icon, I would be questioned at length. What does that mean?"

"We are assuming that Ill Wind and their suppliers are as sick of this as we are," he said. "With part of the icon and you, Ill Wind should be able to negotiate for the detonators, on the understanding they will learn from you where the rest of it is. They will question you about this."

He paused, looked at me, then lowered his eyes. "They will hurt you." He stood and walked over to the window. "The longer you do not tell them anything, the better your chance of survival, but the more they will hurt you."

"But with your sexual problem," interrupted Misha, "I say you will not last two minutes."

"I do not have a sexual problem," I said.

"You do."

"Virginity is not a problem."

"Yours is."

"That's nonsense."

"It is reality, girl. When you meet Achim, you will find out. He will check you the way I did. He will discover where you are weakest, and he will tear you to pieces." He threw up his hands in disgust and walked away. "This is impossible. It will not work."

"It will work," said Vasily.

"How?"

"She must control her fear."

"And," said Louis, "she must not be a virgin."

Misha paused and looked at me.

God, no. Don't look at me that way. You're thinking too much.

"Choose," he said.

Here was an area where I was not lacking in conviction. I might compromise with murder, but never with sex. It was impossible. I would die first. I began to feel virtuous again. I was on firm ground here; I knew what was right and I would not deviate.

"No," I said.

"You must. Choose."

"I will not participate in any way. I'll die first. I will take the first option."

"You picked a fine time to develop a backbone, girl."

I felt Misha's contempt keenly, but not strongly enough to compromise my principles. I stood firm.

"Alex," said Louis. "This is not something to die for."

"There have been many sainted martyrs who died for it."

"You are no saint," said Misha.

"Your life and many others are at stake, Alex," said Louis. "Think of that. God will understand."

"We say that a lot, don't we?" I said. I looked at Louis. "Is that how you live with yourself?"

Louis answered with a glare, an unforgotten glare that has remained between us, separating and binding us at the same time, like a hyphen.

"Enough!" said Misha. "Alex, I will not allow you to jeopardize this operation, nor will I permit you to commit suicide over this trifle."

"Trifle!"

"Yes, trifle. Compared to what is at stake, it is a minor point. You cannot face Achim as a virgin. Choose one of us now or I will choose for you."

"No."

Misha looked to his left. I saw Vasily shake his head out of the corner of my eye, but I could not look at him. There was a very sharp exchange of words between them in Polish. Misha's vehemence bordered on rage, frightening me so that I looked at Vasily involuntarily. His gaze was locked with Misha's in a silent battle of wills, his face set in that expression I later came to know so well: total intransigence.

Misha looked away first, disgusted. "We will use chance," he said. "Do you have any playing cards?"

I would not answer him. The look he gave me sent a shudder through me.

"I saw some in the kitchen," said Louis. He retrieved a pinochle deck from the utensil drawer where I kept it and gave it to Misha.

Misha shuffled the cards and put them on the coffee table before me. "Cut them," he said.

"No."

Another freezing stare. "High card," he said finally. "Louis?"

Louis took the top card. It was a jack. He smiled and gave me a significant look, evidently not knowing it was a low card in a pinochle deck. Louis's jocularity can be deceptive; his true nature is often vengeful and he forgets nothing.

The merest remark can lie buried in him, fertilizing his fury until it grows into a monstrous plant bearing fetid fruit. I know this too well.

Vasily took the next card. It was a king. I breathed a little easier. If it must happen, at least it would be with my love. It began to seem not so bad, compared to the alternatives. I calculated the probabilities. With eight aces available out of forty-six remaining cards, the chance of disaster was less than twenty-five percent. Misha took the next card.

It was the ace of diamonds.

"One more time," said Misha. "You choose, or we go by the cards."

Something inside me was screaming *Say Vasily, Come On Say It!* but I was paralyzed. I was entrenched in my cause, and having chosen, could not go back. That would be admitting defeat. I could not admit defeat, no matter how much I wanted to.

Vasily told me later how hurt he was. He said it would have hurt more to force me from my stupid stand though. But I think if it had worked out that way, I would have relented, and it would have been better for me. People who say they have no regrets amaze me. Have they never done something that hurt everyone and helped no one? Have they never been so sure they were right that they went to the wrong lengths to prove it? Or am I the only one who makes bad decisions when I am ignorant, scared, and confused? Good can come of evil by the grace of God, and eventually, it did even in this instance, but at the time, my ordeal was merely a shabby little drama that disgusted us all.

Vasily and Louis waited in the Mercedes outside.

"I do not understand how an intelligent girl can be so stupid," said Misha.

I suppose he was trying to put me at ease.

"I will do my best," he said, "but I am not gentle. It will help if you do not fight me."

I did not fight. There was no point. Neither did I cooperate. He was right. He was not gentle. I don't think there is anything gentle in him. Even the meticulous manners his aristocratic family took such pains to teach him do no more than muffle his natural abrasiveness. He is a stinging nettle in bloom: beautiful to look at but uncomfortable to brush up against.

Though I found out differently later that night, I thought at the time it was the worst pain I would ever bear. I maintained my composure, though, and when instructed, dressed myself calmly in the short blue skirt and checkered shirt that was to be my outfit for the evening. It made me look as I felt.

"Was that something to die for?" asked Misha.

"No." I hated to admit it.

"Was it worth hurting others for?"

"No," I whispered as my tears started again.

"There are many forms of selfishness, Alexandra. You and Vasily are perfect for each other."

TWENTY-ONE

By the time Louis and Vasily came back upstairs, I was well into a crying fit, a silent one, with wet cheeks and an occasional shoulder shudder. I felt, and probably looked, like a used mop. My hair was a disaster and I stood bare-legged straight because the damn skirt was too short to sit down in.

Vasily said something to Misha. I suppose he misunderstood my tears. If I briefly hoped for vengeance, it was a futile thought. I was new to the dynamics of the relationships within Charlemagne, but it did not take me long to see that there was a bond among these three men that I would not be allowed to disrupt. I began to understand where I stood with Vasily. This did not help my dwindling self-confidence, though it brought a little wisdom. I realized I was not important enough to cause Boris's beating, either. There had to be some other reason for that. Somehow this made me feel better, maybe because it relieved me of my share of the responsibility, however unintentional.

I was important to Vasily, but not in the way I thought at the time. Only many years later, when he began to thaw a bit and when I learned more about his horrific life, did I realize that when I first met him, he was incapable of loving me in the fairy tale way I had dreamed of. Love is an irresistible, selfless giving. Vasily loved me because he wanted me. It is not the same thing.

Hindsight can be comforting, but of course, at that moment, I had none of it. I simply stood, shattered and wretched, in the short blue skirt that made me feel like a whore. I had been violated, albeit with my tacit consent, and was being used ruthlessly, given a minimal chance of survival, a chance one of these men, at least, had argued I should not have. The worst was still to come, and I shivered at the thought of it.

Vasily made me sit down and then sat next to me, miserable heap that I was. He put his arm around me and drew me to him. At first, I resisted, could not bear to be touched, until I gradually understood that he meant to comfort me. I buried my face in his shoulder then, taking the comfort offered, momentary protection and safety in his arms.

He whispered in my ear, "Are you frightened?"

"Why?" I whispered looking up at him. "Do I look it?"

He smiled. "Can you never answer directly?"

"I'm terrified," I admitted. "I am more frightened than I've ever been."

His whisper became barely audible. "So am I. And so are Misha and Louis."

My eyes were wide open at this. "Oh great. Then what chance do I have?"

"Every chance. We are all scared, always. We survive because we do not let fear stop us. We keep thinking and we keep doing what must be done. Does that help you?"

"You're telling me not to panic. Is that it?"

"I suppose."

"So when does the fear stop?"

"In my world, never."

"Then I suppose, I have an advantage. I know a place without fear."

He looked at me with alarm, "Don't do anything foolish."

"I am not talking about death."

"What then?"

"Never mind."

"What?" he insisted. "Your God? I hope he gives you more help than he does me. Or your religion? It did you a great favor, giving you exactly the wrong thing to be prepared to die for."

"Virtue is not a wrong thing."

"Being stupid about sex is not virtue. Sex does not warrant death."

"Sex can feel like death in the wrong conditions."

He looked at me. Did I imagine a softer expression? "Assault is sin," he said. "Not sex."

"No time for theology," said Misha. He handed Vasily a folded pile of black clothing. "Get dressed."

Vasily got up and Misha sat in his place. It was like a wind change, and I shivered in a cold northerly as Misha opened a new make-up kit and began to transform my face.

"For all your piety," he said, "you are no better than me."

"I never said I was."

"Don't talk. You will smear the lipstick. You never said you were, but you think it. Your thoughtlessness can be as deadly as my knife. And can cause more pain."

"You are mired in evil." I said it through clenched teeth, as much in an attempt to keep my temper as to save the lipstick.

"We are all mired in it," he said. "Or did your Messiah come only for my sake and not for yours?"

"What do you mean?"

"Never mind. Philosophy is a luxury of the idle. We have work to do."

My face painted, it was time to do something with my hair. This fueled a debate. The hair was shoulder length with a blunt cut that made style more or less impossible. Louis solved the problem with a side ponytail that brought my mane under control, and a scarf that added color. I was rather pleased with it.

Misha did not like my skirt and used a stapler to tighten it and masking tape to shorten it. Shoes were last—high-heeled and painful.

The men wore black denim trousers, black boots, and black, long-sleeved cotton turtleneck shirts. Over these, sport jackets in different colors drew attention away from the uniform blackness of their clothes.

Why bother? I wondered.

Misha, as usual, read my mind, or my face, or whatever it is he does to know what I am thinking. I have only ever been able to conceal one thing from him in the twenty years I have known him.

He answered the question I had not spoken. "Black makes it difficult to judge," he said. "Achim and Ahmed are big men. We want them to judge our sizes without accuracy. We want to help them make mistakes."

Louis cleaned his gun, meticulously dismantling and rebuilding it. He rummaged through a small box of wires and gadgets and gave me a button-like object to swallow. "A precaution, so we can follow you," he said. "Do not lose it."

Misha gave me more instructions. "Do not lie to them. You do not know or you will not say, but do not lie. Allow them to think you are Grayson's lover, but do not tell them so. They will catch any lies, and from these, they will extract the truth. Make them work for anything you say. Keep the subject on the icon. Give us time."

"Alex," said Vasily slowly, as if uncomfortable with giving advice, "it will help to fix your attention on something you can see, a pattern in a ceiling, perhaps, and try to breathe in rhythm."

"Rest as much as you can," interrupted Louis. "And do not think ahead. Fear of pain is worse than pain itself."

"There are twenty-one distinct levels of pain," said Vasily. "Convince yourself that the last was the twenty-first, that the next will be no worse."

"No, no," disagreed Louis. "Do not think ahead at all."

TWENTY-TWO

Misha drove me in my car, while the others followed in the Mercedes. We spent most of the time in silence, but I ventured to ask a question or two of my own.

"You don't think they will hurt me badly, do you?"

"I know they will."

This took a moment to digest. "How badly?"

"I cannot explain it because you have never experienced it. You have no basis for understanding. That is why you are doing this because you do not know what you are doing."

"I don't understand."

"Exactly. It is the argument I gave Vasily, but he is adamant. He gave you advice. I give you a way out. If you tell them where the icon is, they will simply shoot you. There will be no more pain. It will help us if you wait as long as possible to tell them, but how long is up to you."

"You're not going to come and get me?"

"Yes, we will, but you are not our priority. When it becomes too much for you, you are free to get out."

He parked the car on a dark side street somewhere on the South Side, having driven the last half-mile slowly and without lights.

"Now listen," he said. "Go two blocks, then left. It is on the right. The place is called Rick's. Give me two minutes, then start walking."

"By myself?"

"Yes. There is no danger here. Rick's is a sovereign house. No killing, no exchanges, no secret work, only talk, at Rick's and within the approaches. These extend a little over half a kilometer all around the place. We are within that radius. You can walk to Rick's."

"What is a sovereign house?"

"It is a bar, and sometimes a restaurant, where everyone can go, in some safety, to talk. There are several of these places, in different cities around the world. Inside, it is usually divided into three or more sections. To the right is the West, and to the left, the East. In the center are the neutrals, true anarchists, and the indiscriminate. In countries with more factions, there are more sections. At Rick's, you will find Ill Wind in the center. Just ask the barman. When we come in, be sure you do not recognize us."

"But I'm hopeless. You know that. They will see it all over my face."

"No. They are not that good, and you are not that bad an actress."

"Where will you sit?"

"We do not usually work for the East, for many reasons, not all of them ideological. We will sit on the right."

Rick's occupied more than one building. It was a collection of several small buildings, each built hard against the other. Any spaces between them had been walled up, making the place whole, but all the doors remained. They were painted the same color and matched the paint on the brick walls so well that the structure was a monotony of grey in the moonlight. There was what seemed to be a main entrance, lit by a small neon sign saying "RI_K'S," but this was the only distinguishing mark.

I entered through the lighted doorway, and after descending three steps, found myself facing a long bar that began in front of me and stretched away to my right. Clutching the section of icon hastily wrapped in two brown paper sacks under my arm, I asked a man behind the bar where I would find Ill Wind.

His answer was perfectly bland. He pointed to my right and said, "Third table, down the center."

At the end of the bar another step led down into a large room, filled with booths and tables, but clearly divided into three sections. The room was about two-thirds full. Only a few other women were sitting down, and none of us looked like ladies. The waitresses ran from tables to bar to kitchen, then back to tables.

Traffic between the sections was very free. Animated discussions in various languages took place at most tables, sometimes between tables, and I could even hear a few shouting matches between the sections.

I approached the third table in the very center. Two enormous and several smaller men sat at a table for six. I could not accurately count them because they kept coming and going.

The two big men were quite still. Misha had understated their size. These were giants. Whereas Louis was the only member of Charlemagne who even reached six feet, topping it by only an inch or two, these men were well over that. I estimated six foot four or more. And they had the bulk and the mass to match their height. I tried to convince myself that their girth was probably fat (they looked self-indulgent), but when one of them stood up and offered me a seat in a mock gesture of exaggerated politeness, I could not find evidence of even a spreading middle. He was as perfect and as muscular as Vasily or Misha or Louis, but much, much larger. Things were looking bleak. I began to doubt I was on the winning side.

And they had minions. They had countless nasty little men, little Borises, hangers-on who hovered around the table and eyed me with disgusting glee.

The one I came to know as Achim spoke to me first. "Buy you a drink?" he said.

"Yes, please. Vodka." This had been Misha's instruction. It would be good preparation, he said, without filling me up or making me too stupid.

Achim caught a passing waitress by the waist, pressed her to himself, and ordered my drink. I saw many things in his behavior and felt relieved.

He had straight black hair, an olive complexion, and a full mustache that would have given him a Latin look, but for the large, straight coptic nose that suggested an Egyptian origin. What I saw that relieved me was in his black predatory eyes. He was not much smarter than Boris. Or maybe he once had been, but now his mind was concerned with other things, comforts and excesses, and lacked the discipline to think clearly. He was a voluptuary without discernment and no match for the men of Charlemagne. I observed his brother and to my inexpressible joy found that he, too, was little more than a lesser man in tough-guy form.

"And what can we do for you, little girl," said Ahmed.

"Brent Grayson sent me."

There was immediate interest.

"Yes?"

"He said to give you this." I handed my package to Achim. He seemed to be in charge.

He tore a small section, then ripped the paper off completely. "Where is the rest of it?" he demanded.

"Brent said we should talk about it."

"Why isn't he here?"

"He's indisposed."

"Where is he?"

"At my place, taking a bath." I thought this was clever and was pleased with myself for one or two seconds.

"And where is your place?"

Payment for breaking Misha's rule, "Don't be clever." I was no longer in charge of the questioning. I had to get it back on track before they strayed into more questions I could not answer.

"That's not important," I said. "The icon is."

"And where is that?"

"I'll tell you when we come to an arrangement."

"What arrangement?"

"We, Brent and I, want a better price and some way to hand it over safely." I emphasized the word 'safely'.

"What price?"

"Seventy-five. It cost us more than we expected."

"Forget it."

I stood up. So did Achim. I started to leave, but he took my shoulder, covered it, in fact, with one enormous hand, and held me fast. He looked at me sharply and for a moment I saw the man he once had been or that he might have become, and it frightened me. He was formidable.

"You know where the icon is?" he asked.

This was the crucial question, the point from which I could not turn back. I had been strictly instructed to answer this question with what I thought to be the truth. The operation hinged on it. I had also been told the likely consequences of my answer.

"Yes," I said.

The two brothers spoke rapidly in a language I did not recognize. Achim told me to sit down, took the icon, and disappeared down one of eight shadowy corridors off the main room.

Ahmed began a conversation, obviously working his way to the subject of the icon. He tried several times to get me to reveal where it was, each attempt so clumsy and transparent that I found it hard not to smile as I evaded his question. Ahmed resembled his brother except that I could see no trace of the shrewd mind I had noticed in Achim. He was also in less perfect condition; his excesses had begun to show in his puffy face and swollen middle.

"Do you see those men over there?" he asked.

"Where?"

He pointed behind me and I turned. Vasily, Louis, and Misha were being shown to a table by a fawning waitress.

"Which men?" I asked.

"The ones just now sitting down. Do you see them?"

Yes, I see them you fool and I want to run over there and throw myself at Vasily and beg him to protect me from further con-

tact with the likes of you except that would displease him and
might even kill him so I will put up with you a little while longer.

"What about them?" I said, turning back to Ahmed.

"We are going to kill them—tonight."

That's what you think, you slug.

I pretended to be mildly surprised and impressed.

"You see...," he continued. "Do you see the blond one, the Austrian?"

I turned again and said, "How the hell do you tell who comes from where?"

"The blond one, the one on the right."

"What about him?"

"He thinks he is good with a knife. We know differently."

You know nothing.

"Oh," I said. "And how's that?"

"Look at him! He is half Achim's size. Achim's arms are twice as long...."

Like a gorilla.

"...and he thinks he is smart." Ahmed was still talking. I had missed something. "But he will discover brains are shit against a mountain, eh?"

He roared at his joke. "Now the bomber..." He was suddenly serious.

"Bomber?"

"The one with the messed-up hand, the shortest one."

"They're all sitting down. I can't tell which is shortest, and I can't see their hands."

"The one with light brown hair, like yours."

"Yes?"

"He is the best. He is certainly the best." Ahmed's voice was lowered, his tone respectful. "He can blow up anything. He can place a charge in precisely the right place and in the perfect amount and detonate it at exactly the right time. He is incredible. Everyone agrees. He is the best. It is a pity he will die tonight, too. And the other one. They say he can listen to any conversation. Maybe he is listening now eh? Maybe he has a gadget that can pick up what we are saying right now. What do you want to say, eh?"

"What?"

"What do you want to say to them?"

Get me out of here.

"I think they're kinda good-looking." I took one more look at them.

Ahmed laughed loudly, drawing everybody's attention, including the three I was looking at. I turned away quickly.

"Their women, the ones who live, are high class. Way out of your league, little slut. They say," he leaned toward me like a conspirator, "that the Austrian can cut your throat before you know he's there."

I could see that he was trying to frighten me with the thing that most frightened him. I tried to look frightened. It was not hard to do under the circumstances.

"Why are you telling me this?"

"Because you will die tonight, too." His voice was still low, conspiratorial. "How badly you die depends on how soon you tell us where the icon is, eh? If you are a very good girl, we'll do you a favor and let the Austrian sharpen his knife on you. If he can find us, that is. They say there is little pain."

"I'm leaving." I got up to go.

Achim was suddenly behind me, speaking rapidly to his brother in their language. I was bundled down one of those corridors, protesting uselessly. Nobody paid any attention.

So much for the safety of a sovereign house.

TWENTY-THREE

B esides pain, my memory holds only a few distinct images of that night. One is of a large cream-colored car in which we traveled and in which Achim pawed me roughly as a prelude to what would follow. He must have been satisfied that I was what I appeared to be because what followed was not sexual. Not that I cared much once it began. Still, I suppose Misha was right again. I doubt I could have withstood the psychological pain had it been otherwise. At twenty, my body held more strength than my mind.

I was taken to what I presumed was a basement in the Sears Tower. I had an impression of a very large building and I distinctly remember being forced down flights of stairs. Frankly, I did not care much where I was. My world had become centered on a grey metal case that covered humming ventilation machinery. It made a handy platform, six by six by three feet high, like an oversized, inverted double coffin, where they laid me out to hurt me. There were ducts, pipes, and valves above my head. Bare light bulbs scattered about this place gave light and shadows to more grey-cased machinery and ductwork and the faces of the men who gave me pain.

I saw these things in between the pain when I rested. When there was pain, I saw nothing but a red-painted valve handle above me that I concentrated on.

I came to know in the next few hours that life is not all that is and that losing it is not the worst thing that can happen. I had wondered why Misha said he feared pain more than death and after fifteen minutes in that cellar with Achim and company, I understood perfectly.

It was not just physical pain. It was a loss of everything else. While I hurt, I lost time, memory, mind, heart, and will. I was absorbed by myself. There was only me, a screaming, aching me I did not recognize. There was no time when there had not been pain, and there was no time when there would not be pain. Pain was now; there was only now, I could not escape it, and I could think of nothing else. A voice inside me counseled me, telling me this would end. Eventually, it must end; it could not go on. But I rejected this counsel because I had forgotten everything else. It would never end.

I did not pray. There were no prayers in me. Only pain. I looked down at a dark place within and did not like what I saw. Only the tiniest fraction of my will held onto the hope I had once foolishly boasted I would never lose. Yet that fraction was enough; I survived. More than that, I changed. It was a change that cannot be explained, only experienced.

During interruptions, I rested. I paid little attention to what was said. I did not answer any of the questions they shouted at me. The brothers left at various times and returned, carrying packs of explosives, timers, and detonators. Their suppliers had been satisfied with just the section of the icon and gave them what they needed. They no longer devoted their attention to me and allowed the leering henchmen much leeway in the way they treated me.

It had become pointless and I knew it. The pain was for nothing, and there was no sign of rescue. But I could not tell them where the icon was and end it. I longed for death. I knew it would release me, but I could not be the one to bring it about. I clung to life with white-knuckled determination. I would not let it go while it was in my power to keep it. Life was a pointless misery, but I hung onto it at any cost.

I had long since given up hope of rescue and was resting during an interruption when Achim came into the space where I was held. Ahmed had gone off somewhere—I don't know where—setting charges, I supposed. There were five or six odious henchmen scattered around me. It was a large space divided into sections by machinery cases, supporting pillars, and foundation work. It hummed and echoed.

In the echo, I heard a change in Achim's tone. I felt a change in his manner. I opened my eyes.

"Where the hell are they?" he said to one of the men who sat about ten feet from me watching something in a briefcase. Achim stepped behind him and peered into the case. "They should have been here by now," he said. "Any indications?"

"No. Nothing." The watcher shook his head.

"But everything is in place? All the sensors?"

"Everything." This time he nodded.

"There is no point to this thing if we do not get Charlemagne. Where the hell are they?"

Ahmed came in from a narrow space to my left. "They will be here," he said. "And even if they're not, it will be a nice big bang." He picked up more of what I assumed to be plastic explosives and began walking away to my right.

"The bang is secondary, fool," said Achim. "It will get us nowhere without the primary. Go on, finish, and let's get out of here. They are not coming. Somehow they know."

I felt his attention turn to me. I was careful not to look at him.

"Has she told you anything?"

"No," answered the man whose job it had been to apply pain for the last half hour. "Not a thing."

"Nothing?" Achim stood over me. "Look at me," he said.

I obeyed.

I could see very clearly. It was as if I were looking into his mind. I watched as he began to understand, even as I understood what his plan had been. What little hope I had left faded. This was a trap. Charlemagne knew it was a trap. They were not coming. Achim would shoot me now. Except that he would not shoot me now, I knew, because there was something else in his face.

"You should have told us by now," he said. "You have been coached." His face contorted with anger as he grabbed me by the shirt, pulling me toward him. "Who coached you?"

I had no opportunity to answer him as the man on my left slumped over the machine case I was sitting on, his blood splattered across my legs. The other men were falling also, but it was outside my experience, and I did not understand what was happening. Achim pulled me off the case by my hair and hooked his arm under mine from behind. I heard his knife open and felt it cold against my neck as he dragged me from that place. I did my best to stay on my feet and cooperate rather than test the edge of his knife, but my feet had been injured so he had to drag me as he ran through a maze of machinery and pillars.

I did not realize he was being chased until we came to a cul-de-sac formed by a large packing case, a pillar, and an outside wall. He turned, with me in front of him, and faced Misha.

"I will cut her. She is yours, isn't she?"

Misha's gun was pointed toward us. "She is not mine," he said. "Go on. Kill her."

Well, thank you very much, you bastard.

Achim hesitated, uncertain, and at that moment Misha crossed the ten feet between us. He kicked me squarely in the ribs of my left side. The force of that kick tore me from Achim's grasp and slammed me against the wall. I fell, breathless, and lay insensible for several seconds.

When I could look, I discovered that things were not going well for my side. It is true my side was only the lesser of
two evils (depending upon perspective), and it is also true
that I was not qualified to determine what constituted 'going
well' or 'not going well'. But the point is that I would have
been happier if Misha were the one on top with the knife. As
it was, he was on bottom, the knife was in Achim's right
hand, and Misha's left hand was around the larger man's
wrist, straining to keep the edge from his own throat. I could
not see Misha's right hand, nor Achim's left, but I could see
the faces of both men. Their concentration was total. Only
one would win.

I knew which one I wanted to win. I sat up, looked
around, and tried to think. Misha's gun lay in the corner near
where my head had been. I hadn't the faintest idea how to
use it, but I picked it up. I considered trying to shoot Achim
but knew I would never be able to do it accurately. The gun
was heavy, so I held it by the barrel, crawled toward the two
men, and swung the gun down on Achim's head with as
much force as I could muster, which wasn't very much. It
was so puny that nothing happened. There was only the
briefest distraction.

But perhaps that distraction was enough for Misha. In
the next moment, Achim grunted and heaved, spilling the
bloody contents of his stomach over the right side of Misha's
face and shoulder. There was a pause; then Misha levered
the body away from him, and it fell face up, disemboweled,

knife clattering from its right hand. Misha pushed himself to a sitting position, leaning against the wall, his knife in his right hand. There was blood everywhere, and he was wet with it. I felt sick but empty, and he waited a moment, panting to catch his breath, then held out his left hand as soon as my first bout of heaving had passed. I did not understand at first, then realized I still held his gun. I gave it to him.

"Don't ever touch my gun again," he said. His eyes were ice blue as he glared at me through the grime on his face.

I was too exhausted to be indignant.

I heard footsteps. Misha paid no attention and continued to glare.

It was Louis. "Ahmed is headed out. He has the laser control."

Misha looked up and nodded. He put his gun away and pushed himself up wearily, using the wall behind him for leverage.

"Cover Vasily," he said. "And take her with you."

TWENTY-FOUR

I hobbled, painfully, trying to keep up with Louis as he led me, and sometimes dragged me, through the cellar labyrinth. We found Vasily standing on a six-foot crate, calmly dismantling six small oblong packages of yellow plastic. He worked quickly, his face expressionless. He removed the detonator, the primer charge, and then the explosive, jumped off the crate, and stuffed the bomb into a sack that once belonged to Ahmed.

Louis lifted the sack and we followed Vasily to the next charge. This was in a more sheltered area where we surprised two building security guards who surrendered their guns to Louis immediately. When this bomb was safely in the sack, he and Vasily held a short discussion about the guards. Vasily glanced toward me. There seemed nothing available to tie them, but he dug into the sack and came up with two lengths of wire. Louis snorted derisively as he helped Vasily tie their hands and arms. He kept his gun on them and dragged them along on our quest. At each stop I slumped to the floor, trying to breathe without pain, not succeeding, and finally distracting myself by watching, fascinated, as Vasily worked. As did the guards.

Misha joined us eventually. He gave the laser control to Louis, who took it apart before putting it in his back pocket.

In a short time, though it seemed long to me, Vasily announced that we had come to the last one.

This one was high on a wall behind a pair of crossed girders opposite a small space where the tied-up guards sat. The girders made an X halfway up the wall, each rising in the opposite direction at a twenty-degree angle. The bomb had been placed at the ceiling above the right-hand girder.

I was in a puddle on the floor, still trying to breathe, grateful that this was the final device.

"Hold this, please," said Vasily.

He stood over me, handing me the holster that held his gun. I guessed he had taken it off as a precaution. Unencumbered by the weapon, he easily pulled himself up to the last set of explosives and dismantled it. The immobile guards watched until Misha's sharp look made them turn their heads.

The last charge in hand, Vasily slid down, took his gun from me, and put it back on. He held his hand out, helped me to stand, and supported me on his right arm.

We stood under the girders, finished, but not relieved. Misha looked at me. "Will you be coming with us?"

I knew what he was asking, and I had an answer. He did not say, "Are you coming?" but "Will you?" He wanted to know if I would go with them to whatever lair they might slink to in whatever country that might harbor them.

I had seen enough death, felt enough pain, and shared enough guilt to last my lifetime. I loved Vasily, but I could not have just one part of him. If I wanted him, I must take all of him, as he was, and there was a great deal of him that I did not like. I remembered Boris. Vasily was made of the same fabric as the men who had hurt me that night.

Guilt was another problem. It was overtaking me. I had actively and willingly taken part in a killing. I could not console myself with the thought of the hundreds, maybe thousands, who would live that day. I could see only the awful reality of death in the bodies of those who died in that basement, evil though their intentions had been. I did not know if I had done the right thing. I knew only that I wanted no more decisions like it. Give me moral neutrality, no more questions I cannot answer, no more choices I cannot discern. I am a child of this world, and I am bound to it by chains I cannot break.

I said, "No."

Misha gestured with one hand, with just two fingers of one hand. A minimal gesture. Vasily raised his eyebrows, questioning, as his left hand reached for his gun. He shot the security guard on the right, just above the nose. Louis, who stood to our left, shot the man on the left. Both guards fell at the same time.

I was sick again. This completed the horror. My only comfort was that I would soon be rid of these men. We trudged to the exit, where we stepped over Ahmed's body, slipping in his blood.

The Mercedes had been parked some distance away. My condition slowed our progress. We had not gone far when I could go no further and collapsed on a green space, begging to rest against a tree. There was a brief discussion before Vasily and Misha left to get the car. Louis sat beside me.

"It was a trap for us, you know," said Louis.

"Yes. So I understand."

"We were lucky to have you."

"Pardon me?" I did not want to talk. It took too much breath.

"The sensor you swallowed picked up all their sensors. We knew every wire they used and had to find a way around them all to surprise them. That is why it took us so long." He looked at me. "I am sorry."

For what? For taking so long? Or for dragging me into this in the first place? Waste no apologies on me. Just take me home.

"You have been a very great help," said Louis. "Thank you."

Apologies and thank yous. Just take me home.

"Misha thinks they were greedy, but I think they were cowards."

I could only register my puzzlement in my expression. I had no breath to spare.

"They waited ten days for the lasers," Louis explained. "Misha thinks they were too intent on destroying the building as well as us, but he is wrong. Achim needed accuracy so that he could trap us and detonate at precisely the right moment. He did not want to fight Misha, just kill him. He was a coward."

He paused. "Misha won, anyway."

I nodded at the obvious.

"He did not win easily?"

I shook my head.

"It is always that way. It is always decided in a moment of chaos."

He paused again, then continued, picking his words carefully. "You are important to Vasily. This…"

That was all I heard before I fainted. I woke again in the back of the Mercedes, next to Misha, who stank with a vile odor. It was almost dawn, and we were heading south on the Dan Ryan Expressway. Louis drove, and Vasily sat next to him up front.

Misha's hand was under my shirt, exploring my bruised ribs. "I am sure I broke a few," he was saying.

I pulled away from him.

"You will be all right," he said. "We will take you to your parents' home. Your father will know a doctor to call."

I kept my eyes on the lightening sky outside, fighting the urge to be sick.

"Look at me," said Misha.

I did not. He took my chin and turned my face toward him. I glared at him, telling him exactly what I thought of him without wasting the breath to say it.

"Listen." He was glaring back at me. "Frank will ask you all about it. You must tell him nothing. Do you understand?"

I defied him.

"You will be in great danger if you tell him anything. Do you understand that?"

"What will you do to me?" I asked.

"I will do nothing," he answered. "Frank is a good man, but his organization is a sieve. Nothing is secure. You do not know what is dangerous to you or not, so say nothing."

"I don't know or I won't say, is that it?"

"They will not hurt you. Just say nothing."

Vasily turned and said something I did not catch.

"And burn these clothes before you see Frank," Misha said. "Do it immediately."

Gladly.

Vasily supported me as I struggled up the walk to the front door of my parents' house. We did not speak to each other. He picked the lock and I entered without looking at him. I shut the door between us, locking it with as much noise as possible.

I put on an old bathrobe and lit the fire my father always kept ready. I was watching the fire, watching the last bit of aqua turn to ash, when I realized my father stood next to me.

"Do you need a doctor?" he said.

"Yes, please."

TWENTY-FIVE

Mama fussed over me; the doctor bandaged me. I fell into a comfortable sleep for a few hours, warmly tucked into my old room. I delighted in this comfort and welcomed my mother's attention. I did not welcome Frank's visit, though. My father insisted on staying while Frank asked his questions. My only answer was silence. I was good at this; I had practiced.

"She's tired, Bud," said Papa. "Let her get some more rest before you debrief."

"She's not tired, Fred. She's been coached. She's been told not to say anything. Where's your brain been since you retired?"

"This is my kid, Bud. Leave her alone."

"I can't and you know it. You trained me." Turning to me, Frank said, "Alex, have you been threatened in any way?"

I did not answer.

"Okay. Let's try this. Look at me, Alex. We can pretty well piece together what happened. It's obvious you were there. There's just one thing we can't figure out. Please help us. There were two men, shot right between the eyes. They were unarmed, arms tied. Wearing security guard uniforms. Know anything about that?"

I turned away.

"No. Look at me and listen. This was no accident. Our friend Mack the Knife had to have authorized it, ordered it maybe. Any idea why, Alex?"

I was beginning to think. I did not like where my thoughts led.

"There's always a reason for what he does, Alex. Remember, I told you that a few days ago. Why'd he have them shot? Did they see something they shouldn't have? What could they have seen that would get them shot, eh?"

I remembered their surprised faces when Vasily climbed that girder. *No, not then, before then, before he climbed.*

"They were not what they seemed," I whispered.

"Very good. You're right. They were babysitters, controlling Ill Wind, and supervising the operation. They might have been useful alive. It's not like Charlemagne to waste a source of information. So what did they see that got them each a bullet between the eyes?"

I didn't tell him, but I knew. They saw me holding Vasily's gun. Misha knew who they were when he saw their surprise. But that still did not kill them. The order came after my decision to lead a 'normal' life, to tread the middle ground.

A word can kill. An omission can destroy as surely as a commission. I did not kill those men, but I was bound up in their deaths, and no matter how ignorant, my involvement was not entirely innocent. Until the week before, I had been firmly rooted in the belief of my righteousness. I had suc-

cessfully avoided all the obvious sins. But now I was con-
fronted with the fact that my silliest decisions could have
consequences beyond me, beyond my intentions, and my
control. I was not qualified to figure in so many questions of
death. So who is? Misha? Vasily? The hot-headed Louis?

No. But at least they knew that. While I blithely made
decisions based on my convenience, without regard to consequence, they saw consequence in every move.

My tears began when I thought about Vasily. What an
awful place he lived in. I would not compromise with what
he did, but I loved him, and I stopped judging him. I had a
dismal record in judgment, anyhow.

Since then, I have always distrusted people who are
convinced they are right. We are a confused and befuddled
species, universally so, but too many of us depend on our-
selves for answers to questions we have no business asking.
We can pray for guidance and beg forgiveness, but we cannot depend on the righteousness of man. Earthly judgments
should be made only by people who understand their own
fallibility.

I stopped asking myself questions and sobbed.

"Alex," said Frank softly. "You should have gone with
them. If I can figure it out, others will, my dear. I'm not the
smartest man around. There are bound to be others."

"What the hell are you talking about, Bud?" asked Papa.

"You know what I'm talking about, Fred. You just don't
want to admit it to yourself. Your daughter has access to one

of Charlemagne. It's the only explanation. She has access and she wants to stay home." He stood up to leave. "You can't stay home, Alex. When they come back for you, you'll have to go."

"No," said Papa. "She doesn't have to do anything she doesn't want to do."

Not true, I thought. On the whole, my wants and my have-to's were not matching up. But one want was over-powering: Vasily. I would have to live where that circum-stance put me, pray for guidance, and beg forgiveness.

When Frank left, Papa brought a chair to my bedside, sat down, and took my hand. "Is it the one who was here? Is it Sobieski?"

"Yes, Papa."

I noticed tears in his eyes.

"Your mother's heart will break. She loves you dearly."

"I know. But I love him, Papa."

"Just like she loved his father."

"What!"

Papa looked at me intently, paused a moment, then de-cided I should know.

"I told him one lie, Alex," he said. "His mother was not the only one who had access. His lover, not his wife, chose the boy's life over his. I think she is going to regret it."

It took a moment for this to sink in.

"You let him think it was his mother?" I asked.

"I love my wife, Alex."

"But you..."

"Before you finish, listen to me. I will tell you what I told him when you were in the kitchen. His father was an ace, Alex, and he was the best. Nobody, not even an intimate, can sneak up on somebody that skilled."

"Are you saying he wanted to die—for his son?"

"I'm saying he was a light sleeper. That's all. And before you go explaining things to your lover, my girl, think about the consequences. I've told you this so you will understand it when your mother falls apart and I am left to put her back together."

TWENTY-SIX

Father Paul disagreed with my decision. He told me this many times in the next few weeks.

My physical recovery was quick. Papa's doctor called the school and had my finals postponed. Studying for them speeded my mental recovery, but I felt empty without Vasily. Father Paul assured me this was normal and would pass in time. I moved back to my parents' house and waited.

Frank gave me the entire icon I had taken to Rick's, though it was still in pieces. I don't know how he recovered it. When my feet healed sufficiently, I broke into the church and leaned the pieces against the northern wall. Another miracle. Father Paul did not ask me how I found it, but I could tell he knew I had. I also never told him who took it. I try, during confessions, not to confess other people's sins along with mine.

Father found the money also, where I had hidden it inside the stand that held the icon of St. Sergius. He moved the stand to make room for the ladder he used to replace the Trinity Icon, and there it was, all fifty thousand, in cash. Yet another miracle! The bishop was more skeptical, but after a careful and unsuccessful search for the owner of the money, he distributed it among the churches, giving the lion's share to St. Sergius.

Sarah disappointed Father Paul because, to my knowledge, she never laughed again. He seemed content, though, with the miraculous conversion of Boris, who even assisted in the Liturgy once he could walk again. This I know only second hand from Mama because I left while Boris was still confined to a wheelchair.

It was Boris's first Sunday out of the hospital when Vasily came back for me. That morning the papers were full of news about a fabulous shootout in St. Louis. Father Paul had just pronounced the final blessing when Vasily, Misha, and Louis entered the church.

They were grim-looking men, rather scruffy, unshaven, and disheveled. In contrast, Father Paul faced them calmly with splendor, strength, and power. Boris sniveled in his wheelchair. He had a long way to go yet. Mama began to cry. Papa wrinkled his brow and glowered with bitterness. I saw it all in a moment and ignored their faces from then on because my attention became fixed on my love as he crossed the room and stood beside me.

"Marry me?" he whispered.

"Yes."

"I have an announcement," began Father Paul. "This is Alex's last Sunday with us, and I think it is appropriate that we sing *Many Years*."

"Her last Sunday?" asked Erin. "Where are you going, Alex?"

I could not answer because I did not know.

Louis answered for me. "They are to be married and will live in Europe."

"Married!" This came from several people and was followed by hearty congratulations and questions and comments about my handsome fiancé (and unspoken but obvious surprise at my having landed him). There was a marked lack of enthusiasm among my parents, the priest, and the lump in the wheelchair, but nobody seemed to notice, least of all the Matushka, who was busy trying to welcome Misha and Louis into the church.

Misha gave her a sub-zero stare that could not be mistaken for anything other than active dislike. She was mystified, and I must admit so was I for many years, until Misha explained it to me at your father's funeral.

Misha did not like Erin because he believed she betrayed her husband by hiding the icon. It was tantamount to shooting him with his own gun, said Misha. She had access, and she misused it. I countered with the argument that she did so out of love for her husband. That made no difference to Misha.

Unfortunately, he and I had that discussion because he was accusing me of doing the same to Vasily. You see, both Mama and I were right. Vasily did turn, and when he did, he was dead within five days. Misha accused me of betraying Vasily by causing him to stop defending himself, but I told Misha that I never asked him to. Vasily's work was a No Man's Land that I did not enter after our marriage. It was his decision to leave his gun at home that day, his decision and his obsession. He did it as much for himself as he did for you or me.

He called you his miracle, and as you grew, entombed with the rest of us in the comfort and security of our prison estate, he wanted other things for you, things he knew about only vaguely, what he called a normal life. He was practicing, pretending, trying to experience life without fear, hoping to someday give you that kind of life, wishing it was his.

I miss him dearly.

I still tend to choose life at any cost, even this fearful, constricted life that we've tried so hard to help you escape. I was glad Misha did what had to be done when they tried to kill you with your father. I am only sorry you had to witness such a gruesome thing, especially when you were not yet twelve, and I fully understood your reluctance to go near Misha afterward.

But there is one other thing that I must tell you. I tried to tell your father, several times, but he always prevented me. You were his miracle, and he did not want to know the cause. He was your father in every sense except one, darling, because on that Sunday in Chicago when he came for me, I was already pregnant.

It always amused me that no one else saw the resemblance. I saw nothing but. Even Misha's wife, Katya, remarked on how closely you resembled Vasily, but then she had a talent for self-deception and maybe she was helping to maintain the fiction. I don't know. All I know is that your Slavic features came from me, dear one, but your exceptional beauty came from Misha.

As I look back on it, I think that everybody, Louis, Katya, and even Vasily, knew. Only Misha is truly in the dark about it. I know he is because he mentions marrying you off to his son. I suppose that night in my apartment is a non-event to him, as it can never be to me. Anyway, he has suggested a sponsalia, wanting me to agree to a marriage between you that is not a good idea for more reasons than he knows. I enjoy knowing something he doesn't. It does not happen often. But I thought to arm you with this knowledge just in case.

Your half-brother Michael is a chip off the old block, chiseled from stone, compelling, and doubly dangerous because he has inherited Katya's charm. He took Vasily's place in Charlemagne after his sister and mother were killed. I don't think he is particularly interested in you, but he is an obedient son, so do be careful and use this information if you have to.

It is because of Michael that the recruiters have contacted you. He has taken more responsibility within the team, and has a prejudice against Americans, after the loss of half his family. Frank has not yet retired and is highly placed in his organization, but his organization is still a leaky, loose collection of very smart men who can't keep secrets because they try to keep too many. Michael shuns them absolutely, and Frank wants you to help change Michael's mind. I'd say you have about as much chance of that as I have of converting Misha to Orthodoxy.

Still, there are miracles, and some cannot be explained. I remember something Misha said before we left the church that day, and I left home forever. Everyone else was crowded by the door. He was looking at Sarah, restored to her proper place on the northern wall. He motioned for me to stand near him.

"Do you think she will ever laugh again?" he asked.

"No," I said. "She has seen too many things that are not funny."

"I disagree," he said. "She will laugh again." He paused and looked at me. "But you and I will never hear it."

EPILOGUE

E rin enjoyed this chore. It was quiet. Quiet was a precious commodity and there was comfort here in the
empty church. The Saints, especially the women, commiser-
ated with her as she dusted, polished, and vacuumed. It
went quickly, sometimes too quickly, now that Yelena Dolnikova watched the children for her. It was odd that Yelena
would offer to do that. No one else ever did, as much as Erin
had longed for it, and Yelena had never been a particular
friend.

I suppose she misses her grandchild, thought Erin.
Strange that they should name the baby Mara. Too bad for
Yelena that they live so far away. Still, the one time I met her
daughter's husband and his friends! I have to admit I
wouldn't want them to live too close. Alex always was a
strange one. And I don't care what Paul thinks, that girl had
something to do with the money, she and her creepy friends.
No doubt. I owe her, though, for not telling Paul how she
found the icon. Come to think of it, how did she find it?

Erin was not one to solve puzzles willingly and found a ready distraction in a new carpet burn that required treatment. Boris is hopeless, she thought. Paul insists that he is improving, but I don't see it. He nearly killed my husband when he set his vestments on fire with the incense. I suppose he tries hard, but I wish he'd start succeeding.

She said a short prayer for Boris's success.

She said another short prayer for her husband's rapid recovery.

Paul had suffered a second-degree burn over his lower left leg but did not take it well. Long-suffering was not his strong suit, he told her. She agreed.

"It's a good thing men don't have babies," she said.

"Ooh. Don't start telling me about labor and all that again. Ooh!" He groaned, moaned, and made himself a real nuisance.

"Why don't you try breathing exercises like we did when we had Peter? I'll coach you."

"You'll what? Don't be ridiculous."

"No. Really. It'll help. Come on."

Their concentration lasted almost two minutes as they stared into each other's eyes, breathing in rhythm. Until the laughter began. They accused each other of starting it but once started, it was mutual and simultaneous and overpowering, leaving them helpless in each other's arms, unable to speak, unable to do anything without laughing all over again.

Erin was dusting the Trinity Icon as she remembered this, gently rubbing a smudge from a shiny new hinge on the right side.

She did not realize she was laughing aloud again until she heard the answering chuckle from just above her left shoulder.

The End

Will Alex live happily ever after with Vasily and the rest of the team? Find out in the next file, *Cetus Wedge,* available at your favorite store: https://www.charlemagnefiles.com/linkmap.

Join the Charlemagne Files newsletter for more engaging stories and information about the series, its world of covert operations, and the lives of the characters on the team. Sign up here: https://www.charlemagne-files.com/contact.

If you enjoyed this book, please leave a short review at your favorite bookstore.

www.ingramcontent.com/pod-product-compliance
Lightning Source LLC
Chambersburg PA
CBHW070527260626
47161CB00004B/1647